KERRIE O'CONNOR has been a journalist for twenty-six years. Her career has spanned print and radio and she has won awards for investigative reporting. She left ABC Radio to answer the call of *Through the Tiger's Eye*, the first book in the Telares series. The story had bubbled away since she travelled to war-torn Eritrea to make a series of documentaries for Radio National.

Kerrie was born in the Year of the Tiger and *By the Monkey's Tail* grew big and strong in the Year of the Monkey, sharing a nursery with Kerrie's baby son.

Also by Kerrie O'Connor

Through the Tiger's Eye

BY THE
MONKEY'S
TAIL

KERRIE
O'CONNOR

ALLEN&UNWIN

First published in 2006

Allen & Unwin
83 Alexander St
Crows Nest NSW 2065
Australia
Phone: (61 2) 8425 0100
Fax: (61 2) 9906 2218
Email: info@allenandunwin.com
Web: www.allenandunwin.com

National Library of Australia
Cataloguing-in-Publication entry:

O'Connor, Kerrie, 1962–.
By the monkey's tail.

For primary school aged children.
ISBN 978 1 74114 405 5.
ISBN 1 74114 405 1.

I. Title.

A823.4

Designed by Jo Hunt
Set in 11.5 on 15 pt Berkeley by Midland Typesetters, Australia
Printed by McPherson's Printing Group

10 9 8 7 6 5 4 3 2 1

Contents

Before you begin

1 Kissing Carlos the Criminal 1
2 Lucy's Confession 5
3 Nigel Bulldozer 12
4 Tigerish Reunion 17
5 That Hunting Feeling 21
6 Old Enemy 27
7 Carpet Runners 32
8 Mango Magic 37
9 Old Friends 42
10 The Rebel Base 47
11 Dream Weaver 51
12 Nigel in the News 56
13 Planning 63
14 Children of Letters 71
15 Angel Insists 77
16 Night Adventure 82
17 Holding Hands 88
18 Catastrophe in Kurrawong 95
19 'Angel Won't!' 99

20	The Easter Bunny	104
21	Teaching Tiger	111
22	Carlos' Ordeal	118
23	Raising the Roar	124
24	Tigerish Tricks	129
25	Tunnelling	135
26	Great Balls of Fire	141
27	Old Man River	149
28	Adrift on the River of Souls	153
29	Taken	157
30	Mud People	161
31	Mango Monkey	164
32	The Journey	168
33	Houseboating	174
34	Pasadena Square	181
35	The Secret of the Rug	188
36	Family Dramas	200
37	Monkey Magic	206
38	Trashcan Trap	211
39	The Rescue	215
40	Going Home	225
41	Another Goodbye	228
42	Nigel's Undoing	233
43	The Document	236

To our golden monkey, Atticus Panckhurst

With thanks to: Melissa, Nina and Helena, for hanging in there. Sarah Brenan, for surgical steel. Eva, for turning the map the other way up. Erica, for fabulous phone-side manner. The Brunette Aunties, for various monkey business as deadlines loomed. Oscar and Sam, for advice and patience, and Gabriel, for sharing his exams with baby primates – and all three for being awesome big brothers. Lakota Ullrich, for her painting. Joan Hornig, Aveen Beedles and the children of letters at St Therese's – and all the kids, teachers and librarians who welcomed a tiger and asked for more. The wonderful people at Holding Education for their support. The welcoming staff at my local RSL for giving me a quiet place to write. And, for wit, wisdom and kindness in the jungle, my abiding gratitude to Michael Panckhurst.

Before you begin

Last summer, when Lucy and Ricardo and their mum moved to the Mermaid House, they found a way to another world. A mysterious Tiger-cat showed them a secret tunnel leading to a country called Telares.

In the jungle of Telares, Lucy and Ricardo discovered a terrible injustice – children chained up and working as slaves for the Bull Commander. Bull soldiers had invaded Telares and renamed it East Burchimo.

Meanwhile, back at the Mermaid House, the strange tiger carpet in their room seemed to be growing itself alive, and Nigel Scar-Skull was causing trouble. His aunt Nina Hawthorne, the owner of the Mermaid House, begged Lucy and Ricardo to protect her precious dragon chest. Somehow the chest was linked to the rug and to the future of Telares.

Lucy and Ricardo risked everything to rescue their new friends from the Bull Commander. But then they had to say goodbye, as Rahel, Toro, Pablo, Carlos and Angel headed for the safety of the mountains. Their job isn't over yet, though . . . as you will see when you read By the Monkey's Tail.

1
Kissing Carlos the Criminal

'Hey, Lucy! Is your boyfriend still in jail?'

Laughter burst from the back of the bus, where Blake Richards sat with all his jerky Year 9 mates. Up the front, Lucy smouldered, trying not to explode.

'Just ignore them,' hissed Janella. Then she went back to gazing out the window, as if the wire fence around Kurrawong High School were the most fascinating thing she had ever seen. Easy for Janella, thought Lucy, knuckles white on her soccer bag, as another round of guffaws rolled up the aisle.

There was only one thing to do: she would have to arrange for Ricardo to be kidnapped. Again.

The first term of high school had been great – until her jerky little brother Ricardo got talking to Blake's jerky little brother at primary school. In a quiet moment, feeding the school rooster, Ugg Boot, Ricardo had blurted out everything about Telares. Well, not *everything*, he assured Lucy later. Not the part where Lucy and Ricardo had travelled down a weird time tunnel to get there, with a bit of help from a mysterious half-cat, half-tiger who could not only beam video clips into their brains but also talk. He wasn't *that* dumb.

What he did confess to saying, before Lucy dunked all his Spiderman comics in the bath, was that he and Lucy had flown to another country called Telares for the Christmas holidays and they had met some kids. One of them was called Carlos and he was a boy and he was Lucy's friend. What was wrong with that? Oh yeah – and Carlos was in jail.

'Well, it's not true, so I didn't do anything wrong,' he had argued with his usual twisted logic. 'Carlos isn't in jail any more and we didn't fly to Telares.' He opened his mouth to continue, but something in Lucy's face made him gulp and finish lamely, 'So it's all good.'

All good? Lucy had first felt the impact of his big mouth the following Monday morning, on the bus, when Blake struck up a chorus: 'Lucy loves a criminal! Lucy loves a criminal!' By recess it had spread through Years 7, 8 and 9; by lunch, the whole school. By 3 p.m., every boy on the bus (along with a few of the girls) was singing Blake's tune.

After an excruciating few days the novelty had worn off a bit. Most of Year 7 was bored with it, or had started to feel sorry for Lucy, or had shut up when she and her soccer team cornered them at recess. Only Blake and his back-seat mates kept it up, but today was the last day of term, so Lucy just had to get through the trip home and she wouldn't have to see any jerks (apart from Ricardo) for two weeks. Besides, if she turned around and said anything, it would only make matters worse.

'Hey Lucy! What's it like kissing Carlos the criminal?'

Lucy turned around and said something. Actually, she shouted it. 'He isn't a criminal!'

The bus fell quiet. Even the driver swung his head, and Janella looked at her piercingly. Oops. Lucy remembered she had denied knowing anyone called Carlos.

Blake's words stabbed the silence like a poison dart.

'But you did kiss him?'

The bus erupted. His mates were high-fiving and hooting. Janella tried to stop Lucy jumping out of her seat, but she was too late.

'Oooh! Look out, Blake. I think you made her mad,' a chorus crowed as Lucy strode up the aisle. But something about her expression as she bore down on them caused some to giggle a little nervously. Lucy ignored them. Her eyes were fixed on Blake, who was pretending to hide behind the guy next to him. A familiar thunder was building in her feet and it took all her control not to let it boil up into her chest and erupt.

Blake, acting terrified, peeked out from behind his mate's shoulder – and froze. Lucy had stopped half a pace away, eyes blazing. Suddenly, he looked confused. He didn't move, or laugh, the way any normal Year 9 boy would if he was threatened by a mere Year 7 girl. All his mates watched. Lucy leaned closer, not taking her eyes from his. Every cell thundered, but still she held back, battling to stay within her own skin.

Blake paled, shrinking into the seat. Lucy saw goose-bumps on his arms. She leaned closer and saw fear in his eyes. A centimetre closer and she saw panic. She waited until he knew that she knew he was scared – and all his mates did too – then she growled two words: '*Back off!*'

The stunned faces of all the back-seat boys gave her a particular feline pleasure. Lucy shook herself and stalked back down the aisle to flop next to Janella, who was gazing at her with both admiration and disbelief.

'What did you say to him?'

'Just told him to back off,' Lucy said casually – but her voice had a curious purring timbre.

'But . . .'

Lucy followed Janella's gaze back to where Blake and the others sat, strangely subdued.

'But how . . . ?'

Janella gave up.

'Weird!'

As the driver fired up the engine, the only person tempted to sing was Lucy.

2

Lucy's Confession

Janella had never been to the Mermaid House – but she was about to make up for that by staying for the whole Easter holidays.

'Cool!' she exclaimed, thumping the knocker – a mermaid's scaly bum – on the heavy wooden door. She didn't seem to notice how old the house was, or how wobbly the verandah. Thank goodness Mum and Grandma had done such a great job tidying the front yard. Instead of a jungle, it was now a proper old lady's garden, with roses blooming over the archway (disguising the fact that they were actually holding it up) and bright flowers lining the path.

Lucy escorted her friend up the mermaid carpet to the ballroom, T-Tongue bouncing at their feet. Janella was blown away.

'Wow! Let's have a party here.'

Stripped of the layer of dust that had once cloaked them, the ballroom and its polished grand piano were awesome. Painted sea creatures swam on walls, floor and ceiling, as though you were walking underwater.

'Fantastic! Why didn't you bring me here before?'

Lucy blushed. She didn't know how to say she had been too ashamed, ashamed about Mum and Dad breaking up and about living in a daggy old house, even if it was weirdly cool and she loved it.

Just like Lucy and Ricardo the first time they saw the house, Janella could not resist turning on all the bathroom taps to watch water cascade from the brass dolphins' mouths. She admired the stained-glass starfish in the windows, before falling in love with the fierce dragons emblazoned on tall vases that guarded Lucy's bedroom.

Lucy was suddenly quiet. She opened the red, carved door and formally invited Janella in. This was her room now, so it was clean-ish. Ricardo, to his utter disgust, had been banished with all his junk to a smaller room. He'd thrown his biggest tantrum in years, but for once Mum had stuck up for Lucy, insisting she needed her own room to study in now that she was at high school.

Janella stepped onto the tiger rug. Would she notice?

'Wow!' Janella fell to her knees and Lucy couldn't restrain a giggle of delight as her friend began to stroke the mane of the midnight-black horse in one corner of the rug. Except for a white star on its forehead, the horse was so dark that it almost vanished into a patch of woven night sky. It had appeared only in the last few days, very faint at first, and Lucy almost hadn't dared to hope – but now she was sure. The rug was growing itself alive again, and so was the stubborn hope she would see her Telarian friends soon. Cool! Life in Kurrawong just wasn't the same after everything that had happened over summer. Even the excitement of going to high school did not make up for the loss she felt whenever she thought about Telares. Which was weird, as Telares was dangerous – Ricardo had almost not made it home from there, and if he hadn't it would have been *her fault*.

That mysterious horse meant a lot to Lucy. It meant her adventures were not just a dream. And her friends – Rahel, Pablo, Toro, Carlos (yes, Carlos) and tiny Angel – they were real and out there somewhere.

'What do you see?' Lucy asked Janella softly. But Janella's face, as she continued to stroke the carpet horse's mane, had a faraway look, as though she were seeing something so compelling she had forgotten her surroundings. Suddenly, her fingers whitened as she gripped the horse's mane and her eyes grew large. Blood drained from her face and she began panting as though she were running hard.

'Janella!' Lucy was alarmed.

Shuddering, Janella pulled her hands away from the rug and sat up straight.

'Whoa!' she whispered.

'What? Tell me!'

Janella spoke breathlessly. 'I can't believe it! The horse is real! I could hear him in my mind. He liked me stroking his mane and he was whickering to me, he wanted me to scratch his forehead and between his ears.'

'Cool,' said Lucy, with a touch of envy.

'But then – I was riding him!' The words came out in a gallop.

'Riding!'

'It's true. I was riding bareback and he, the horse, was

galloping and I had to hang on really tightly or I would have fallen off. And we were running from something dangerous.'

Lucy felt the room grow cold and almost didn't dare to ask.

'What were you running from?'

'I don't know. The horse did, though.' Janella looked anxiously at Lucy. 'I can't explain it. He spoke in my head. I know it was a he. He told me to hold on tight because there was danger.'

Lucy wasn't sure what to say. She knew all about danger. Telares had shown her things she never wanted to see – children chained up and forced to work as slaves, making soccer balls and rugs in the Bulls' horrible jungle jails. She'd seen the Bull soldiers' cruelty and violence.

'Where did you *get* this carpet?' Janella breathed. She tentatively ran her fingers through the glorious tiger's fur, carefully avoiding the snake entwined between its front paws.

'It was just here,' Lucy said.

Janella shot her that look, the one that said, 'You're not telling me something – and I'll get it out of you, sooner or later.' The same way she had, finally, after a week of high school, got Lucy to admit that something *was* up, that Mum and Dad had split. And suddenly, after telling Janella, it still wasn't great, but it didn't feel so bad.

Lucy struggled with the urge to tell Janella everything. But she had promised the Telarians she'd keep their secret. The battle must have shown on her face because Janella took a deep breath and rammed her advantage home.

'And who's this Carlos you lied to me about?'

Lucy went bright red. 'I didn't,' she said lamely.

'Yeah, right!' Janella raised her eyebrows. 'Spit it out.'

So Lucy did.

It was hard to describe her Telarian friends. First of all, Rahel might be the same age as Lucy, but she definitely wasn't normal. Her life was too psycho for that. But she was as calm and still as water – until anger unleashed a storm and she did what she had to do to defend the people she loved. Then there was Pablo, who never got angry, even when he should. And annoying Toro, who at least kept even-more-annoying Ricardo occupied. And tiny Angel, mute, black-eyed Angel, who was bound to Lucy in her very dreams. And finally Carlos, who was angry most of the time – but Lucy had come to understand why, after a while.

It was even harder to describe Telares itself. More than anything, Lucy wanted to show Janella that mysterious country. But the tunnel that led there was blocked. Lucy often checked, just in case, but it had remained stubbornly closed since the day three months ago when her Telarian friends had helped her rescue Ricardo from the clutches of the Bull Commander. It felt like a year ago. Now there was only a smooth red-and-ochre clay wall where the tunnel opening had been. No rubble or broken beams like dinosaur bones, no hungry tunnel mouth leading under a mountain to another world, a world that you should really only be able to get to by flying across the Pacific Ocean. Telares – floating right on the International Date Line. A place of danger, held captive by the Bulls, who had invaded with their guns from powerful Burchimo.

Not only had the Bulls stolen the country, they had made slaves of its people, the proud Telarians. Families had been torn apart, and sent to far-flung corners of the island as slaves. The Bulls even kidnapped children, as their little fingers wove fine carpets and sewed the best soccer balls. That's what had happened to Lucy's friends. When she found the way to Telares, she just had to help them. Together, they had defeated the Bull Commander and freed every child in the jungle jail.

It took hours and a family block of chocolate to tell Janella everything, chiefly because Janella made her say everything that included Carlos twice. And Lucy couldn't help explaining twice how she had paralysed the Bull Commander with her tigerish roar, saving Ricardo and Rahel.

Janella sat up.

'So that's what you did to Blake today!' she said accusingly.

'Kind of, but I held back. I could have gone further,' Lucy said darkly. She collapsed on the tiger rug, too exhausted to explain further. But there was something she had to know.

'You don't think I'm crazy, do you?'

'I always thought you were crazy,' Janella said helpfully, lying across the carpet horse.

'Thanks! But seriously, do you think I'm nuts?'

Janella held her gaze candidly. 'If you had asked me before I went for a ride on Dark Star here, I would have said you were absolutely nuts. But that ride was freaky! So, if you're crazy, so am I. That carpet does something weird to your brain.'

'Lack of food will do something weird to your brain,' said Lucy's mum from the door.

Lucy caught her breath. How much had she heard?

But Mum looked perfectly relaxed. 'Dinner's ready!' she said cheerfully.

Afterwards the girls stayed up late, watching movies and eating even more chocolate and telling Ricardo just why he should never, ever tell Blake's little brother anything about anything again. When they finally stumbled into bed, it was to strange dreams – followed by an extremely rude awakening.

3

Nigel Bulldozer

'I'm going to bulldoze this dump!'

Lucy had almost forgotten how much she disliked Nigel Scar-Skull. One sentence was enough to remind her.

What a way to wake up! Lucy and Janella were sleeping in after their movie marathon when someone started hammering at the door. And that someone was Nigel Scar-Skull. Did he have to show up every school holidays? It was Easter Sunday the day after tomorrow, but Nigel sure didn't look like the Easter Bunny.

He kicked one of the verandah's wobbly floorboards. It jiggled precariously. 'See, the place is dangerous. Pity it didn't burn down in the bushfire last January. It ought to be demolished – and that's just what I'm going to do as soon as my aunt's death certificate is signed.'

Lucy stopped rubbing sleep from her eyes and stood bolt upright in the doorway.

'What do you mean, death certificate?' she squeaked.

'I'm sorry, Louise,' said Nigel, who didn't look sorry at all. 'Someone has to tell you. My aunt, Mrs Hawthorne, is missing. I put her in an excellent home with the best medical care, but they said she spent all her time talking to a cat. Then she wandered off a few weeks ago and no one has seen her since.'

Nigel looked positively elated, but Lucy felt as if her heart had stopped. Nina Hawthorne owned the Mermaid House and, if anyone could, she owned the Tiger-cat too. Lucy wasn't quite sure how the old lady was connected to Telares, but she knew it was important. And she knew Nina was afraid of her nephew, Nigel.

'Nina,' was the only sound Lucy could squeeze out.

Nigel stepped closer, frowning. 'Mrs Hawthorne to you, Loretta. And don't think I don't know about your little visit to the nursing home.' His face had grown quite red. 'My deluded aunt told you to hide that dragon chest of hers, didn't she?' He moved even closer and Lucy had to make herself hold her ground.

Janella, clearly a little nervous, emerged from the hall in her pyjamas to stand beside Lucy, who shot her a look of immense gratitude. Lucy immediately felt better. Her sense of security increased tenfold when she registered a telltale brush of fur on her legs. T-Tongue had doubled in size in the past three months. Now, with every hair on his back standing up, he looked formidable. He growled ominously and Nigel took a step back, then looked over his shoulder as though fearing an attack from another quarter.

Lucy's spirits rose. Nigel was a bully and a big liar. He was just saying Nina was dead so he could get the house and the dragon chest. And Lucy knew exactly why he was now rubbing a set of shiny scars on his bald skull. She wasn't going to tell him she hadn't seen the Tiger-cat in months. The day she had said a wrenching goodbye to her Telarian friends, the Tiger-cat had deserted her too. But Nigel didn't need to know that.

'My name's Lucy, Neville,' she said innocently, 'and I've already told you I don't know anything about a dragon chest.'

Then she gasped, as Nigel pulled something awfully familiar from his pocket. He dangled it in front of her nose.

'See, I've got the key to the silly old chest. My aunt gave it to me just before she disappeared. She wanted me to have it.'

Lucy couldn't breathe. How could Nigel have got hold of Nina's precious filigree key?

'Pretty, isn't it?' gloated Nigel. 'I can't tell you how many people want this key – so as soon as you hand over the chest, I'll lock them both up nice and snug in my safe.'

How had he got that key? Lucy racked her brains. The last time she had seen it was in the Bull Commander's grasp at the jungle jail. He'd caught her trying to rescue Ricardo and torn it from her neck. Then, in all the commotion, it had been left lying in the dust! The Bull Commander must have returned and found it. But could he have sent it to Nigel? Did that mean Nigel knew Lucy had been in Telares? Did he know about the tunnel? Lucy stared in dread at the man before her.

'I'm telling you . . .' a red-faced Nigel began impatiently, and Lucy began to relax. He was not acting like a bully who had been let into a magical secret – he was just an ordinary bully. The Commander didn't even know Lucy's name, let alone anything about Kurrawong. Besides, the whole story was just too crazy.

Lucy was immensely relieved – and then something cheered her up even more. A creature – small, lithe and dangerous – had materialised at the bottom of the stairs, eyes locked on the key Nigel still brandished. The Tiger-cat!

'I need that dragon chest, Lucretia, and I know you're hiding it from me.' Nigel was blissfully unaware of his nemesis creeping up the stairs, golden eyes now fixed on the back of his skull. 'But you can't hide it from me forever, you know. This house and everything in it will be mine as soon as I get my aunt's death certificate . . .'

At the word 'death', the Tiger-cat launched itself into mid-air. By the word 'certificate' it had landed on Nigel's back and was clawing up onto his head, yowling and screeching like a banshee.

It was all over in a matter of seconds. Nigel took off with a blindfold of ginger fur over his eyes, tripped on the top stair and tumbled to the bottom. The impact sent the Tiger-cat flying, but it was on its paws again before Nigel could move. He lay sprawled on the path, the bloody tracks of fresh scratches on his bald pate, as the Tiger-cat stalked towards him, ears flat, letting loose a terrifying yowl that made even Lucy cringe.

Nigel scrambled up and ran for his car. As his tyres screeched into a desperate U-turn, the Tiger-cat's yowl became a purr and she began rubbing against Lucy's legs. T-Tongue gave a pleased whimper and crept out, quivering and shaking, as though asking permission to make use of his famous Tyrannosaurus tongue. Which was extremely odd behaviour from a puppy who now towered over the feline in front of him. The regal Tiger-cat deigned to sniff the enormous puppy's nose once and then ignored him.

'I guess that was the Nigel you told me about?' said Janella, but Lucy didn't answer. She was gazing after Nigel's car and the big, ugly sign on its roof:

VOTE 1
NIGEL ADAMS
THE NEXT MAYOR OF KURRAWONG

The man who wanted to knock down the Mermaid House was aiming to rule Kurrawong too! And he still had Nina's key. And it was her fault.

4

Tigerish Reunion

Biff! The Tiger-cat's paw batting her cheek stopped Lucy brooding about Nigel's ugly lies, his ominous sign and her own failings. There were the chalk-and-charcoal stripes, far bolder than on any normal ginger cat, and those distinctive round ears with their white spots on the back. Perched on the verandah rail, the Tiger-cat might purr like a suburban moggie, but she was nothing of the sort. (Lucy maintained that the creature was a girl, whatever Ricardo might say. The truth was, neither of them had been game to check.)

The Tiger-cat turned golden eyes on Lucy, who instantly shivered. That extraordinary feeling she'd first experienced on the morning she had found the tunnel engulfed her – a strange aching and then it was as if she simply stepped free of her skin and was one with the air, floating, anchored only by the golden rope that joined her mind with the Tiger-cat's. She watched, awed, from outside her body as the familiar stripes of the Tiger-cat's face blurred and shifted and she found herself gazing into a dark pool of water that rippled and resolved into . . .

the black, black eyes of Angel. 'Lucy must take Angel home. Lucy promised. Lucy will take Angel home. Now!'

The shock of hearing the four-year-old Telarian speak sent Lucy shivering back into her skin. As though it had happened just yesterday, she remembered the dream where Angel's mother had urged Lucy to look after her little girl. *'She is yours now,'* she had said, just before the Bull soldiers dragged her away. A note squeezed into her daughter's hand begged for Angel to be returned home to her grandparents in Telares City.

Lucy stretched out an urgent hand to the Tiger-cat. 'Since when can Angel speak? What happened? What else does she say?' But the Tiger-cat streaked up the nearest tree, sending a burst of parrots into the bright blue sky. Supremely satisfied, she sat washing her face on a fat branch.

'Lucy, you're talking to a cat,' broke in Janella. 'Now I know you're crazy!'

But Lucy was in another world, grinning like a fool. The Tiger-cat was back, with a brand-new video clip of Angel, which could mean only one thing: life was finally about to get interesting again. And Nina wasn't dead, whatever her creepy nephew said. Nina would never let Nigel kick them out of the Mermaid House, or bulldoze it. And somehow, Lucy would get the key back. And no one would ever vote for Nigel to be Mayor of Kurrawong – not even if he gave everyone a free Ten Star Jumbo soccer ball!

Would they?

Mum's Mazda farted and belched into the driveway and Lucy ran to meet it. Ricardo exploded from the car almost before it stopped, eyes riveted on the Tiger-cat. He turned

18

to Lucy, a silent question blazing in his eyes. Lucy nodded – and he let out a whoop that Dad probably heard all the way from his conference in Indonesia. Ricardo opened his mouth but Lucy shook her head, with a warning glance at Mum, who had her head buried in the Mazda's boot.

'Lucy and Janella, would you give me a hand here?' Mum asked. The girls each grabbed four bags of groceries and stumbled in the front door as Ricardo, the Tiger-cat and T-Tongue disappeared at top speed out the back and up the path into the rainforest. Typical! Lucy wanted to drop the shopping and follow, but she couldn't exactly leave Janella to put everything away.

As soon as they'd finished, Lucy ran into her room and grabbed her joggers. Yikes! She almost dropped them again. That golden monkey on the carpet that Ricardo kept insisting was his – Lucy could have sworn she saw it wink! She blinked and looked again, but it was just a carpet monkey, albeit much brighter and more silky-soft than a carpet creature had any right to be.

'Janella, check this out!'

'It's brighter than yesterday,' Janella agreed wonderingly.

Anticipation mounting, Lucy scanned the creatures in her carpet menagerie: the glorious tiger, the creepy snake, the big-eared bat, the elephant with a blood-red jewel on its trunk, and the glorious new black horse that Janella insisted on calling Dark Star.

Suddenly, Lucy was as impatient as a horse herself. She galloped up the hall, into the back yard, up the path, past the chook shed and onto the forest track, with Janella in hot pursuit. There were the stone stairs they had discovered last summer, climbing to the edge of the deep pit that concealed the tunnel to Telares. At the sight of the Tiger-cat perched on the top stair, that familiar hunterish feeling rose through the soles of her feet, into her very bones.

T-Tongue quivered with excitement and Ricardo's face glowed. Lucy didn't need to be told. The tunnel to Telares was open.

5

That Hunting Feeling

The Tiger-cat leaped in a graceful flash of orange to the floor of the pit. With an excited yelp, T-Tongue followed. Ricardo grabbed the rope that had hung useless for months from the tree above and swung down effortlessly. But Lucy paused on the top step, surveying the pile of rubble and broken wood that marked the entrance to the tunnel. Suddenly, she was back in the dream she'd been having when Nigel Scar-Skull woke her this morning. She had been on the steps above the pit, filled with a hunter's urgency – but she hadn't been Lucy, she had been a cat! A big cat.

Without thinking, Lucy crouched.

Hurry!

Blood, bone and muscle answered and she flew into the pit and, without breaking stride, padded swiftly towards the tunnel. Only Ricardo's startled face made her realise what she'd done, and she stopped short. She looked up and saw Janella open-mouthed with shock. The Tiger-cat's expression was unreadable as it perched on a broken beam near the tunnel mouth, but those golden eyes never left Lucy.

'That was awesome!' Ricardo whispered.

'You'll kill yourself one day,' warned Janella.

Lucy examined the pit's sheer walls and understood their amazement. She remembered how much jumping off the roof had hurt when she was seven. She'd broken her ankle and couldn't play soccer for the rest of the season. Yet the walls of the pit were almost as high and she had barely felt the impact – in fact, it felt as if every muscle in her body begged for more.

She shrugged.

'I dunno. It just felt right. And last night I had this weird dream. Anyway, you're getting pretty wicked with that rope yourself,' she told Ricardo, glad to change the subject. Ricardo was flabbergasted. He wasn't used to compliments from Lucy. But it was true. Ricardo had bounced down the walls with the agility of a professional abseiler – or a professional monkey. Most kids his age would have been too scared to try.

Lucy looked up at Janella, hesitating on the top stair.

'Are you ready?'

Janella was quite pale, but she nodded slowly.

'You don't have to come.' There was a hint of challenge in Lucy's tone.

'Try to stop me.'

Janella, fearless on the soccer field, climbed down gingerly.

'Let's go,' said Lucy. But the Tiger-cat lashed her tail as Lucy padded closer. Those golden eyes held hers and, once again, Lucy shivered outside her body and fell into darkness . . .

into Angel's black eyes. 'Lucy will . . .' But before Angel could finish her words, Lucy was rocketed backwards and upwards, as if she were looking down on Angel, floating somewhere above the little girl's head. Lucy had bird's-eye vision – and the view was . . . terrible!

'No!' Lucy cried, rocketing back into her body, heart thumping. She spoke urgently to the Tiger-cat. 'What's she doing there? How did she get there?' But the Tiger-cat vanished with a growl into the mountain's hungry mouth.

'What?' asked Ricardo and Janella, alarmed.

'Angel. She's on her own, right near the jungle jail in Telares. We've got to go!'

Lucy leaped into the tunnel and felt the hunter in her take over, every sense stretching to listen to the darkness. She was relieved to realise her Telarian talents were intact. Even in the deepest dark, she knew exactly where she was. The sonic skill that had been buzzed into her brain, on that fateful day when she and Rahel had first led Angel, Carlos and Pablo into the tunnel and right into a storm of bats, had not worn off. And neither had the thrill of knowing that, after touching the Tiger-cat, she could walk, see and smell like a cat. Although an enormous python slithering over her foot had not been pleasant at all, the gift the snake had given both Lucy and Rahel had already saved their lives. They could sense trouble approaching through the vibration of the earth itself. How cool was that?

It was a different story for Janella.

'I can't see anything,' her shaky voice said, somewhere behind Lucy.

'Sorry!' called Lucy, and meant it. She remembered how

scary it had been the first time she had gone down the tunnel. She went back and took Janella's hand. 'Just follow me. I told you I could see in the dark. Well, it's not really seeing, but I can find my way. It's more like listening so I don't bump into things.'

'Well, you'd better not bump me into anything,' said Janella in a slightly stronger voice. 'This tunnel had better be safe or . . .'

Lucy slowed down to Janella's pace, all the time stretching her mind to sense when they reached the fork in the tunnel. At the fork, she automatically took the right-hand path, the one that sloped upwards to the miners' cubby that the children had claimed as their own. She could hear T-Tongue sniffing and snuffling excitedly up ahead. Soon, they were passing the cubby door. It would have to wait. Angel needed her.

They trudged deeper into the mountain, Janella dragging a tentative step behind while Lucy, exhilarated despite the urgency of her mission, felt her questing senses stretch and grow stronger. Soon they reached the cavernous cathedral where a thousand bats roosted. She decided against sharing this news with Janella. She smiled at her friend's gasp of relief when, some time later, they rounded a bend and met weak sunlight struggling through a maze of vines and creepers onto the dusty tunnel floor. The entrance to Telares!

The Tiger-cat leaped towards the apparently impenetrable green barrier. Vines as thick as iron bars untwisted like spaghetti and fell away, and welcome sunlight spilled into the tunnel. Lucy blinked, dazzled by the unexpected light and the vivid green of the Telarian jungle. She caught

Janella's awed expression and remembered just how she'd felt the first time she'd seen it.

Ricardo wasn't feeling sentimental. 'Get moving!' he ordered, trying to push past.

'Oh, no you don't!' Lucy retorted, grabbing his arm. 'Remember what happened last time? You're staying here. I'm not letting the Bull Commander kidnap you again! Do you know what that was like?'

'Well, duh!' Ricardo was indignant, and loud. 'It was me who was kidnapped, wasn't it? I think I would know what it was like!'

'SHHH!' Lucy hissed. She wanted to screech. It was very hard to fight with your little brother at a whisper, but the jungle could be crawling with Bull soldiers. 'I mean, do you know what it was like for us? For Mum and Dad and Grandma? And me? They wouldn't listen to me. They thought I was crazy! And do you know how hard it was to rescue you? So you're not going!'

'Well, if you hadn't left me out, I wouldn't have got kidnapped. You should have taken me with you and looked after me. So it was your fault. Besides, I have to find my monkey and you can't stop me.'

For once, Lucy was speechless. The worst thing was, she knew he was right about one thing. Short of tying him up, she couldn't stop him going into Telares.

She looked about for some rope.

Ricardo wasn't always silly. 'I promise I'll do whatever you say in Telares, if you don't leave me behind.'

Lucy looked him full in the eye. 'Whatever I say?'

'Yep!'

'Promise?'

'Promise!'

'Say it out loud.'

'I promise I'll . . . '

'SHHH! NOT THAT LOUD!'

'I promise I'll do whatever I say . . .'

'Ricardo!'

'I mean, whatever you say in Telares.'

'You'd better! And Janella's my witness.'

Janella nodded and Lucy took a step into the Telarian afternoon. This time Ricardo wasn't ready.

'Now you say it!' he demanded.

'What?'

'About not leaving me out.'

'Oh, that. I promise not to leave you out.'

'You'd better not. Or my monkey will fight you!'

A low growl gave Lucy goosebumps. The Tiger-cat had heard enough bickering. Lucy shook herself, and stood up straighter. Then, leading the others, she padded obediently along the narrow, twisting path towards the jungle jail, following the white spots on the back of the Tiger-cat's ears, with T-Tongue at her heels.

6

Old Enemy

The kids gazed over the Tiger-cat's head at a desolate scene: the jungle jail, now derelict. It was a copy of the Mermaid House, only more dilapidated. The hungry jungle had invaded, creepers stretching up and over the razor-wire fence, so it was now collapsing under its burden of green. The greediest tendrils snaked up the iron bars that still guarded every window of the house. But the bars were pointless now that the front door hung drunkenly open from its hinges. Tiles were missing from the roof and the verandah sagged alarmingly. The once-formidable jail was deserted, rotting in the jungle's tropical heat.

Lucy almost abandoned caution and stood up but the Tiger-cat, as if reading her thoughts, turned, growled warningly and sniffed the air. Lucy did the same and her cat's nose was overwhelmed with the distinctive scent of smoke. Horrified, she looked around. The wind stirred and then Lucy saw it – a puff of smoke from the old fire pit in the clearing outside the jungle jail's fence. Someone had been there recently! But who? Angel or someone else?

Lucy touched the others warningly and dropped to the ground, her snake sense stirring through her palms. There! The vibration in the earth was unmistakable: heavy boots, marching this way.

'Someone's coming!'

Ricardo didn't question Lucy's urgency. He shrank down as much as he could and even T-Tongue dropped flat. But Janella had no idea what was going on. Lucy dragged her down unceremoniously into the dirt. 'Bulls!' she hissed. Janella's eyes widened and she swallowed a ragged breath.

The shuddering intensified. Lucy dared to lift her head slightly. A man in the distinctive brown uniform of the Bulls had walked into the clearing and stood smoking a cigarette, gazing through the crooked fence. He turned, and Lucy's stomach lurched. She shrank back down. The Bull Commander himself! She could just make out enough to know that he wore the insignia of a black bull with red eyes and yellow horns on his breast pocket, and the vivid scars that gathered one side of his face into a permanent leer were unmistakable. Lucy noticed something else as well: one arm hanging stiffly by his side – a legacy of the last time he had tangled with a tiger.

A slight movement alerted Lucy to the Tiger-cat at her side. She was a porcupine of fur, tail and back arched, fury etched in every muscle. Her golden eyes were fixed on the Commander. If looks could kill . . .

Suddenly the Commander shivered and stamped out his cigarette. He sniffed the air like a predatory dog, his eyes raking the jungle around the clearing. Lucy held her breath. Had he heard them? Smelt them? Felt the Tiger-cat's fiery regard?

Then he did something unexpected. He ran screaming at the wonky fence and shook the wire violently. The gate creaked open, listing to one side, but the Commander didn't seem to care. He threw his head back and shouted something unintelligible to the heavens. He kept hurling what could only be abuse at the sky, until he dropped to his knees and gave Lucy another shock by starting to sob. Then he stumbled to his feet and ran from the clearing, in the direction of the village.

Lucy looked to the Tiger-cat for a clue but she had recovered her sleek, inscrutable persona and merely gazed impassively back. Lucy put her hand on Janella's shoulder and said, 'I think it's OK now.'

'Who was that?'

'The Bull Commander. But I think he's lost the plot.' The sight of her once-terrifying enemy wretched on his knees had given Lucy a burst of confidence and did a lot to make up for how bad she felt about losing Nina's key. At least the jungle jail was not a jail any more and the Bull Commander no longer looked as if he were in command of himself, let alone anyone else. And she couldn't help thinking that she and her Telarian friends could have had something to do with both those outcomes. Elated, she stood up – and almost fell over. A tiny figure had emerged from the door of the jungle jail and was standing in plain view on the verandah, looking straight at her.

Angel!

Lucy was moving before she knew it, loping down through the last stretch of jungle. She raced across what was left of the clearing and through the gate. In a few strides she was at the stairs, taking them three at a time, but the little girl had disappeared into the darkness of the abandoned house.

'Angel!' Lucy hissed urgently, taking a cautious step into the hallway. 'It's dangerous to be here. We have to leave now!' Suddenly she had the creeps. Every terrifying memory of this place and all the bad things that had been done here flooded back. She shivered, taking another wary step. At the gentle brush of fur on her leg she patted loyal T-Tongue's head gratefully. 'Thanks, buddy.' Then she squared her shoulders and stepped onto the first worn-out mermaid on the hallway runner. There was only one place Angel would be.

It seemed to take forever to reach the end of the hall. The door was ajar and creaked mournfully at Lucy's touch. A shaft of sunlight shone into what would have been her bedroom if she were at home, illuminating a giant wooden frame. Stretched on it was the half-woven twin of the carpet in Lucy's room. And it seemed to Lucy's heightened senses that the black horse woven into one corner with the white star on its forehead was gazing at her challengingly. The sun also shone on the bowed head of the little girl who sat on the floor, carefully tying a silky black thread into the tail of the horse. On her lap, coloured threads spilled from a sack.

Lucy stepped inside, looking from Angel to the carpet and back again. Angel tied off the thread and looked calmly at Lucy.

'Angel, didn't you see the Bull Commander? I can't bear to see you here again. What if he caught you? You must come!' But Lucy couldn't help demanding, 'And, anyway, what are you doing here?'

The only response came from behind her.

'My horse!' said one voice, astonished.

'My monkey!' said another, triumphant.

Exasperated, Lucy ran to pick up Angel, but the little girl struggled from her arms, snatched up a pair of silver scissors and began cutting the brown jute that bound the carpet to its frame.

'Angel! There's no time for that, we have to go.'

Angel didn't appear at all concerned about the risk she was taking. The tiny girl just shook her head at Lucy's words, smiled, and kept snipping.

7

Carpet Runners

Half an hour later, Lucy, Janella and Ricardo were sweating and struggling up the track from the jungle jail, desperately trying to keep a grip on the rolled-up rug as they headed for the tunnel. The Tiger-cat had disappeared but Angel skipped about them, grinning like a lunatic.

'Angel seems to have a mind of her own,' said Janella, panting.

'That's her,' Lucy scowled. The tension of finding Angel in the jungle jail, abandoned or not, so close to the Bull Commander, nutty or not, had finally got to her. She had tried to talk Angel out of taking the carpet but the little Telarian had just looked at her with those big black eyes and Lucy had stopped arguing and started helping. She didn't understand why the carpet mattered so much. All she knew was that it was important enough for Angel to trek alone through the jungle to get to it.

But even only half-completed, it was horribly heavy, and the day was hot. They made very slow progress and soon Ricardo dropped his end of the bundle and demanded a rest. Lucy grumped at him but was secretly relieved to sit under a shady tree. She took a sneaking pleasure in seeing Janella look at her watch, and then up at the sun, high over their heads – and shake her head, bewildered. As ever, the Telarian sun was much stronger, and much higher in the sky than it would have been in Kurrawong.

'The time difference takes some getting used to,' Lucy tried to reassure her friend. 'It's hard to believe, isn't it?'

'No choice,' said Janella, shaking her head at her watch again. 'That place was freaky. Was that the jungle jail, where they kept the kids?'

'Sure was. You should have seen them. They were so scared and hungry, chained up like dogs. All Angel had to wear was a torn sack. But not any more! We won. Did you see the Bull Commander? He's really lost it!' Lucy's elation returned tenfold.

'But what's the story with the carpet?' asked Janella. 'Why is it only half-finished, and why was Angel weaving my horse?'

'I don't know,' said Lucy. 'The horse definitely wasn't there three months ago. We rescued the kids before they could finish it. Besides, they didn't have the proper pattern. But we do! It's in the dragon chest. Nina told us to hide it from Nigel Scar-Skull.'

'I don't get it,' said Janella. 'What's so special about a *picture* of the carpet? Why doesn't Nigel just take the real thing from your room? And what has his aunt got to do with it?'

Lucy pondered. 'Well, I bet Nigel can't even see all the animals. None of the adults can see the new animals –

except maybe Nina. Mum still wants to burn it. It's just an ugly old thing to her. But to us . . .'

Lucy would never forget the shock she felt when she realised the rug was growing itself alive in her bedroom, or the morning she had swung her feet out of bed into luxurious tiger fur and fled from the creepy cool of snakeskin.

'But can the Bull Commander see the animals on this one?' asked Janella.

Lucy had never thought about that. 'I don't know. I guess he can. He was the one making the kids weave it.' She frowned, trying to work it out.

A shudder underfoot tore Lucy away from her ponderings. With a bolt of fear, she remembered where she was. The Bull Commander might be a wreck but he wasn't the only enemy they had in Telares. The vibration came again, this time closer. She grabbed Angel's hand, put her finger to her lips to warn the others, and stilled T-Tongue. Where had it come from? Yes, there it was again. Stealthy footsteps, behind. Someone was sneaking up! Lucy cursed herself for losing concentration. She wasn't in Kurrawong now. What was the point of having snake sense if you didn't use it? But it was too late for self-recrimination. The shudder became a quake – and a brown-shirted figure hurtled from the undergrowth. The Bull Commander, once again in command of himself!

'Run!'

They took off, the rug forgotten, as the Bull Commander raised his gun. But brave T-Tongue flew like a black avenger at the foe. Lucy heard a scream and a thump, and turned in terror to see T-Tongue charging back to her, barking triumphantly. He had given them time. The other kids were precious steps ahead, zigzagging through the jungle so as not to give the Commander a clear shot.

Frantic thoughts clashed in Lucy's mind. First, they were in deep crap. Second, it was her fault. Third, Mum was going to murder her for being late. Fourth, so were Janella's parents. Fifth, if they knew who she was, Angel's family would too. Sixth, the Bull Commander had the best chance of any of them – of murdering her, that was.

Lucy, desperate to catch up with the others, put on a burst of speed but her ponytail caught on a branch, bringing her to a crashing halt. As she struggled, a chunk of hair was wrenched from her scalp. In her pain and panic, she was suddenly furious. Her chest boiled. Without thinking, she turned to face their pursuer. Ten steps away, the Commander bore down on her. But Lucy's change of direction disconcerted him. He skidded, raising his pistol in his good arm. In that second of hesitation, Lucy's eyes gripped his and the boiling in her chest became a rumble – and a roar.

It was as if the Commander had hit an invisible wall. His gun was aimed at Lucy's chest but it was useless. His body was frozen. Lucy saw fear in his eyes. Then she *was* the roar. Muscle, blood and bone answered the call and she leaped for his throat . . .

. . . And missed! Mid-leap, she watched the Commander hit the ground, felled like a tree. Lucy landed on all fours where he had stood and shook her head, confused. The rank stench of sweat and fear filled her nostrils. The

Commander was lying next to her, still as death. Had he fainted? There was an insane screech and Lucy almost fainted herself. Then, from nowhere, a sharp blow to her head sent her spiralling into blackness.

8

Mango Magic

Lucy came to with T-Tongue enthusiastically licking her face. Ricardo was saying loudly, 'She's awake!' and someone, not Janella, agreed with him. Who? Lucy opened her eyes to see an anxious face peering into hers.

'Carlos!' she croaked, but his face snapped out of view, replaced by that of a golden monkey. She closed her eyes again until a calm voice said, 'She will recover.'

Her eyes snapped open. 'Rahel?'

'Correct!'

Then Lucy was stumbling to her feet, drinking in a sight that she'd thought she might never see again: Rahel, Carlos and Pablo. And stepping out from behind a tree, Toro, clutching a familiar plastic sword. And swinging up into the nearest tree, not one but two small golden monkeys, clutching – what was that? Mangoes? Yes, green mangoes.

Lucy fingered the bump on the back of her head. 'Did those little suckers throw a mango at me?'

'Sure did,' crowed Ricardo.

'I must apologise for the behaviour of my friend,' said Toro. 'Please accept my sincere regrets.'

Toro? Not only had he grown taller, he'd started to talk just like his big sister, Rahel.

'No worries, Toro. You can't control Ricardo,' said Lucy, 'Don't even try.'

'I refer not to dear Ricardo but to my new friend,' said Toro grandly, gesturing at the nearest monkey.

The bad news took a moment to sink in.

'Oh,' said Lucy flatly. 'A monkey.'

'Correct.' Toro was almost bursting with enthusiasm. 'My golden monkey.'

As if it understood every word, the monkey scampered down the tree and climbed up Toro, burying its head in his shoulder.

There was a pitiful shriek and the other, identical monkey followed. But it ignored Toro, throwing itself at Ricardo like a long-lost friend.

'Yeah, and this one,' said Ricardo with a distinct tone of *Na, na, na, na, na!*, 'is mine.' The monkey wrapped golden arms around Ricardo's neck and hid its big dark eyes from Lucy's disgusted gaze.

Lucy closed her eyes in mock despair. Then she remembered the Commander. She jumped and looked over her shoulder. Everyone laughed. He was lying where he had fallen. Not one but a pile of hard green mangoes and squashed golden ones were littered about him, and his face and hair were anointed with a squishy golden paste.

'Good shooting!' said Lucy admiringly, looking at the monkeys with new respect. Then she ducked as Toro's monkey took aim at her and fired with deadly accuracy.

Toro remonstrated in Telarian and his monkey cringed theatrically. Then it clambered up a tree, hanging its head as though deeply ashamed.

There was an unmistakable giggle from the bushes.

The reaction of the Telarians was instant and urgent.

'Angel! Is she with you?' Mass personal jinx.

'Yes, she was at the jungle jail. Alone. And she made us lug the stupid carpet. But we dropped it.'

Carlos dived under a bush and emerged with a grinning Angel. All the Telarians mobbed her, examining her for injuries. Rahel turned gratefully to Lucy. 'She ran away from our rebel base in the mountains on Sunday. We have been trying to find her ever since. The Tiger-cat told us to come back here.'

'Same here,' said Lucy. Then she remembered who else she was responsible for. 'Oh no, Janella!'

To her enormous relief, her friend stepped from the trees. She looked so out of place in this setting, in her fashionable hipster jeans and midriff top, her long blonde hair loose about her shoulders. But fear had made her eyes a darker blue, and her face was streaked with dirt. Janella said 'Hi' shyly to no one in particular and then sat down beside Lucy and checked out the bump on her head.

'You OK?'

'Yep. It was you I was worried about. I should never have let you come here.'

'You couldn't have stopped me,' Janella said. 'You never have.'

That was true. Janella might be the prettiest girl in Year 7, but she wasn't a wuss. She had fought for her place in the soccer team, along with Lucy. She wasn't loud like

39

Lucy, but she was determined. 'Stubborn as a mule,' her dad said, when she insisted on playing soccer instead of keeping up with ballet as her mum wanted.

'This is Janella, my best friend,' Lucy announced, suddenly anxious about the Telarians' reactions. She had promised not to tell anyone about them. But the Tiger-cat liked Janella – didn't that mean something? And she could see Lucy's carpet.

The group stood silently. Rahel was very still, weighing up the situation. She met Lucy's eyes appraisingly, but there was no mistrust in her gaze. Pablo had his head down, scuffing the ground uncomfortably, but every now and again he snuck little sideways glances at Janella – just like every guy in Year 7!

Carlos was the big surprise. He walked right up to Janella and offered his hand.

'I am Carlos. It is my pleasure to be introduced to you.'

What the . . . ? What had happened to hostile Carlos? – the angry guy who didn't trust anyone and blamed every kid who wasn't a slave of the Bulls for his troubles? Lucy had had to risk her life before he accepted her as a friend. Janella blushed and shook Carlos' hand. Then Lucy got another shock: Carlos looked over Janella's shoulder into Lucy's eyes – and winked! They must have been doing personality transplants at the rebel base.

But now wasn't the time to try to work Carlos out. Even with her head still spinning, Lucy was thinking clearly. She had underestimated the Bull Commander once already and there was no guarantee his men weren't around here somewhere. She did not want to make the same mistake twice.

'We'd better get out of here. And Angel has gone all stubborn about the carpet. We've got to take it with us to the cubby in the tunnel. We dropped it back down the track somewhere.'

'We'll get it,' said Rahel firmly, examining the bump on Lucy's head.

'I'll show you,' said Janella and strode off. Both Carlos and Pablo disappeared after her before Lucy could get up. Rahel met Lucy's eyes candidly, laughed and followed them.

Lucy, her head pounding, sat a safe distance from the Bull Commander, willing him to remain unconscious. Just as they staggered back, carrying the carpet on their shoulders, he gave an awful groan and opened bleary eyes.

The kids took off, Carlos dropping the carpet to scoop Angel into his arms, leaving the others to stumble on with it as best they could. Janella grabbed Lucy's arm and helped her stagger down the track. A terrific screeching overtook the jungle. Lucy turned as a storm of forest fruits hailed down on the luckless Commander. He flailed, slipped, took another direct hit to the skull – and dropped like an overripe mango.

It could turn him off fruit salad for life.

9

Old Friends

The cubby was just as Lucy remembered it. It was full of mysterious shadows and was cold as a grave but the bright candles cheered it up. The musty lounge was still in the corner and the table and chairs stood as they had left them in the centre. Ricardo's face glowed in the candlelight as he watched the golden monkeys munching Toro's supply of mangoes and bananas. Every few minutes they consented to cuddles, clinging like babies to Ricardo and Toro. Then they would screech and demand to be returned to the pile of fruit.

Lucy shook her head in exasperation at Rahel.

'How long has this been going on?'

'Long enough,' said Rahel, smiling ruefully. 'Toro dreamed a mother monkey had been shot and her two babies were lonely, and the next day . . .'

'The next day I walked in the jungle and my monkey threw a mango at me,' butted in Toro exuberantly, as though it was the best thing ever.

'Cool!' Ricardo endorsed this point of view.

Looking at everyone's laughing faces, Lucy finally accepted that she wasn't dreaming. Her Telarian friends were back! But they looked different – bigger and stronger, their faces smoother and happier, even in the shadowed cubby. Toro was no longer skin and bone and he had grown taller. The teenage Telarians had grown heaps taller, but so had Lucy, so that was OK.

Pablo's grin was the same, lighting up his round face. As for Carlos, his features had filled out, losing that pinched, sharp look. He smiled once, quickly, at Lucy and looked away. He still held his body like a taut catapult, but he seemed so much more relaxed as a person. His shoulders were broader, and so far he hadn't coughed. Maybe they really did have doctors at the rebel base, as Rahel's Aunt Larissa had promised?

Rahel's hair was still twisted up onto her head, but someone had plaited it carefully into many ropes. Compared to last time, she looked neat, if a bit grubby. Her jeans and T-shirt weren't exactly new, but they weren't rags.

Lucy checked out Angel last. She wasn't as skinny as before, but she was still tiny compared to other kids her age. Her hair used to be a matted thatch, but now it was clean and tightly plaited like Rahel's. In place of the hideous torn sack that Lucy remembered, Angel wore a little tracksuit. It was remarkably clean for a little girl who had just spent days trekking alone through the jungle, probably living on nothing but ripe mangoes. She looked like a different girl, except for those unmistakable black eyes which, as usual, gazed at Lucy intensely.

Lucy had a sudden flashback to the very first time she had seen Angel – in that psycho dream, even before they had moved into the Mermaid House. Angel had been at a picnic with her mother, wearing a glorious party dress, all ruffles and lace. With a stab of emotion, Lucy wondered whether Angel's life would ever return to normal. Would she be grown up before she got to wear another party dress? How long before the invading Bull soldiers left Telares forever and all Lucy's Telarian friends found their parents again? Her gaze settled on Carlos. It was way too late for him. The Bulls had seen to that. How did you ever get over your parents being *murdered*?

Lucy caught Rahel's eager smile across the table, and realised the Telarian was really pleased to see her. That felt good. It was such a different friendship to the one she had with Janella. They didn't share the usual everyday things that girls share – sport, clothes, school, videos and parties – and Rahel was usually so serious. But Lucy knew that Rahel was a real friend. She'd stood by Lucy when Ricardo had been in trouble. She had used all her seriousness to help free him from the jungle jail – to her own cost. Lucy would never wipe the image of the Bull Commander stamping on Rahel's wrist.

Toro was chattering like a monkey about the rebel base and Ricardo was plying him with questions. Lucy threw off her dark thoughts and listened closely as all the Telarian kids fell over each other to answer. Lucy was suddenly intensely curious. She couldn't decide what to ask first.

Rahel caught her eye, smiled and spoke in her formal, careful style.

'It is very pleasing to see you, my friend Lucy. We have much to tell you.'

'It is very pleasing to see you, my friend Rahel. I have much to ask you.'

There was a split second of silence when Lucy wondered if they would get the joke – and then everyone cracked up. She shot a quick look at Carlos and saw him grin, nothing like Carlos the Zombie of old.

An insistent hand tugged at her jeans. Angel was looking up at Lucy and her lips were moving.

'Shhh!' cried Lucy. 'She's talking.' She bent down to listen, but although Angel mouthed urgent words, no sound came out. Frustrated, Lucy looked to the others for help, but everyone fell silent and their smiles disappeared.

'She still does not speak,' Rahel said sadly.

'But I've heard her – twice,' blurted Lucy. 'One was only in a dream, but the other one was this morning when the Tiger-cat beamed a video clip to me. Angel said I must take her home.'

The Telarians sat up straight.

'On Sunday, the Tiger-cat came to the rebel base for the first time!' Rahel said. 'We could not believe it! And then, that night, Angel ran away. That is why we are here. The Tiger-cat came back and warned us. She showed us Angel at the jungle jail working on the carpet again. We tried to get permission to follow – but the rebel leaders said no. We could not make them understand. They were not impressed by dreams and thought we were hallucinating when we tried to tell them about the Tiger-cat sending messages. Even Larissa!'

Rahel was clearly disappointed in her aunt. Lucy could empathise – she knew just what it was like to confide your crazy life in an adult and have them disregard you. She wouldn't go there again in a hurry.

'It was exceedingly frustrating. We knew exactly where Angel was, but the leaders said we could not possibly know, and besides there was no way Angel could walk that far. They kept searching close to the base but we knew it was useless. So we sneaked away. We will be in very much trouble when we return.'

'Why did Angel run away?'

'We don't know!' Rahel, Toro, Pablo and Carlos cried together.

'Lucy will take Angel home,' said a small voice.

Stunned, everyone turned.

'Lucy will take Angel home,' the little girl said, more strongly this time.

'Maybe,' said Janella, who had less reason to be surprised at Angel's vocal ability, 'it's got something to do with Angel wanting Lucy to take her home. Just a guess.'

10

The Rebel Base

The Telarians also had news of the Bull Commander. Rahel took a great deal of pleasure in telling Lucy what Larissa's rebel spies had found out.

'We heard he has gone crazy with shame. To be defeated by children is very demeaning and the Bull generals laughed at him publicly and made him close down the jungle jail after we all escaped. He is still a commander, but they say if he makes one more mistake he will be stripped of his rank. So, whenever he can, he keeps going back, hoping to catch us again. He believes foreign children helped the prisoners and are hiding nearby. He has made it his personal mission to trap them.'

Everyone had a good laugh about that. But Lucy still had a million pent-up questions. 'What have you been doing? What's it like up at the rebel base? How did you sneak away? Did Carlos get to a doctor?'

'Yes, indeed,' said Carlos proudly. 'We have a hospital, but not like any hospital you have ever seen.' In the candlelight his face was intense, but without the surly expression and anger Lucy remembered so well. 'The base is in a secret valley, high in the mountains. The Bulls have searched and searched, but always they become lost. The Tigers often find hungry Bull soldiers wandering in the forest and chase them all the way back to Telares City.'

'Tigers?' asked Lucy.

'That is the name of our rebel organisation. The Telares Tigers.' Carlos sounded immensely proud.

'Just like your favourite soccer team!' Lucy exclaimed.

'Yes. And we will fight like Tigers until the Bulls are gone. Then we will fight like tigers on the soccer field,' said Pablo excitedly.

It was great to see Carlos and Pablo grinning. Lucy had a vivid memory of the day in the rainforest clearing when she had first heard the story of the Telares Tigers soccer team. It was exciting, but tragic. Carlos' father was the coach. He had stood up to the Bulls and they had paid him back by killing him and Carlos' mother. They had thrown Carlos in jail.

Lucy watched the same memory wash over Carlos' face and, for an instant, he was sullen again. Then he shook his head, as though to dispel the ugly thoughts, smiled briefly at her, and went on with his story.

'The Bulls are going crazy because they cannot find us. They are still paying disloyal Telarians to join the Bull militia, and they send them into the mountains to try to track us down. But the militiamen are very superstitious. They come from the coast and are terrified of the mountain spirits. At night we sneak up on them and scare them, pretending to be ghosts. They wet themselves!'

Ricardo and Toro burst out laughing. Lucy remembered how superstitious Ponytail Zombie and the other militiamen had been. They were terrified to stay overnight in the jungle jail and the Bull Commander had had to force them to do it. They were so scared that they all became very drunk. And Ponytail had thought Lucy was a ghost! Lucy had felt no sympathy for him – until she found out he was actually a spy for the rebels! He wasn't a very good spy because he drank too much wine, but at least he was on their side.

'What about Ponytail Zombie? Is he still drunk?'

'No!' everyone said at once.

'Larissa will not let him drink at all,' said Rahel. 'He has become quite sensible and is our friend. But he was still very upset that we were coming to see you, Lucy. He was the only one who believed us about the Tiger-cat, but he shakes when we mention your name.'

Carlos made a great show of being afraid of Lucy, before ploughing on. 'We Tigers are strong in the mountains, very strong.' His face darkened. 'The Bulls know we are up there somewhere. They have bombed all the valleys. But we have dug tunnels into the mountains where they cannot harm us. We stay underground all day, even for school.'

'School!' exclaimed Lucy. Surely a war should be an unbeatable excuse for not going to class?

'Yes,' said Rahel firmly, with more than a hint of satisfaction. 'We have proper teachers and they insist we go every day. We have doctors, nurses, chemists, builders, everything we need – even,' with a sideways smile at Lucy, 'hairdressers!'

'Cool!'

Rahel was too excited to stop. 'And we have factories, underground. We have generators to make electricity. We make shoes – look!' She put out a foot, clad in a sandal that looked as though it was woven from black plastic. 'Manufactured from old car tyres,' she said proudly. 'But the best thing is the hospital. Our doctors and nurses operate underground! They have saved many lives. You would not believe it, Lucy, it is clean, like a real hospital, and they had the medicine Carlos needed to stop coughing!'

Carlos looked a little embarrassed, so Lucy tried to change the subject. 'But where do you get everything you need? You can't go to the mall.'

'Smugglers,' said Pablo proudly, 'and pirates!'

'Pirates!' said Lucy and Ricardo together, for entirely different reasons.

'Sshhhh!' said Rahel, a little anxiously. 'We are not supposed to talk about it.'

'Yes,' said Carlos, with a touch of his old darkness, 'it would only take one traitor to give away the location of our base, and the rebel army could be destroyed.'

Everyone shut up for a while, but Ricardo could be relied on to fix that. 'Can we go to your base today?'

Toro nodded enthusiastically.

Oh no! Lucy was in trouble. She couldn't have Ricardo trotting off after Toro into a war zone. Ricardo was guaranteed to draw attention to himself before they were a quarter of the way to the Tiger base.

Help was at hand. The monkeys set up a tremendous shrieking as the Tiger-cat strolled into the pool of candlelight and leaped deftly onto the table.

11

Dream Weaver

Everyone greeted the Tiger-cat with delight, but Angel was by far the most excited. She stroked it and everyone fell silent as that powerful purr filled the cubby. Lucy became pleasantly relaxed, as though a warm, sweetly scented breeze had refreshed the stale subterranean air. She blinked, trying to keep her eyes open. Everyone was rubbing their eyes and yawning.

'I'm so sleepy,' Lucy heard herself say from a long way away – and then her head slipped inexorably onto the cushion of her arms and she was . . .

in the tunnel, every sense awhisker in the darkness. Here's the fork – but a stubborn force is drawing her in the wrong direction! She's stumbling on heavy stone legs, as some dark planet drags her into its orbit, its gravity commanding, her muscles no longer her own. Down, down, down, the wrong tunnel plunges ever deeper. The air is cold and there's the irresistible scent of water, then damp, gritty stone under her questing fingertips.

Her feet drum on smooth flagstones leading below to where the tunnel opens into a cavern and a strange dim light fills the air. There's a set of stairs with black water swallowing the last step, slapping and lapping at her feet. A wooden boat is moored to a stake, its rope creaking in protest as the river, flowing out of the darkness, tries to tear it away.

And where the river flows, so too must Lucy.

Lucy swam up through a dark tunnel towards sunlight – then she realised the light was really the Tiger-cat's shining eyes. She shook her head to clear it and blinked. Everyone else appeared to be in the same bleary state. Carlos was rubbing his head as though to make sure it was still connected to his neck. Ricardo and Toro were stunned into silence. (That was an improvement.) Rahel and Janella were frowning, as though trying to remember something that kept slipping away. Strangely, Pablo wore a half-smile, as if a sweet realisation had dawned.

Angel, however, was supremely relaxed and alert. The little girl wore an odd, knowing expression as she considered Lucy, while with one hand she stroked the Tiger-cat, who had begun washing its face and ears delicately as though nothing had happened. Maybe nothing had?

'Did you . . . ?' Lucy started tentatively.

Slow nods from everyone, even Ricardo and Toro, confirmed that she wasn't crazy. She wasn't so sure about Pablo's mental state, though. His half-smile became a lunatic grin as he began cavorting about the cubby. 'The Tiger-cat has revealed the River of Souls!' he chortled. 'That is how we will travel to Telares City. It solves all our problems. We will travel in under the nose-rings of the Bulls!'

Watching him leap about, Lucy decided the monkey disease was contagious. He tried to stand still, but couldn't help hopping every few sentences.

'You must listen to what I am saying. I dreamed of a river. It is the River of Souls, I know it! My parents worked there. I almost grew up in a canoe.' (hop, hop) 'It flows underground from Mount Katerina, right through Telares City, to the sea. Don't you see' (hop, hop) 'what this means?' he appealed. 'The Tiger-cat has shown us the way to take Angel home to her grandparents in Telares City. There is a tunnel and a boat ready for us. We don't have to walk through the jungle!' (star jump) 'The Tiger-cat is looking after us. What is wrong with you all?' He sat down on the floor, suddenly deflated.

Lucy looked at him in consternation. It was totally out of character for Pablo to be so fired up about anything other than beating the Bulls in soccer or on the battlefield.

Rahel nodded slowly. 'I believe Pablo is correct about the River of Souls.'

Pablo stood up on one leg, nodding furiously, which caused him to overbalance again.

'It is where Telarians release the little carved boats that contain the ashes of their loved ones,' Rahel continued. 'They take them into the river caves and set fire to them. The boats are carried under the mountain and out to sea. And he is right also that the river will bear us directly to the heart of Telares City much more quickly than we could walk. We could sail down it to Telares Harbour, or row across it to the centre of the city. This fork in the tunnel, do you know where it is, Lucy?'

'Of course I do. Remember when we came back from the

Mermaid House in Kurrawong? We came to a fork. To get back to the cubby we took the tunnel that sloped upwards. The other one goes deeper into the mountain. We have never explored it.'

Angel's little-girl giggle became a chuckle, and then a full-bodied laugh that made the monkeys shriek and hide under the table. And, of course, nobody understood what she was laughing at and she seemed to have no intention of explaining. She just bounced up and down on the roll of carpet. But that reminded Lucy of something.

'Hey, Nigel Scar-Skull showed up again at the Mermaid House this morning and he's still after the dragon chest. He wants the pattern of the carpet so much! I think he's planning to give it to the Bull Commander. And he's trying to say Nina is dead. And he's running for Mayor of Kurrawong *and* he wants to kick us out of the Mermaid House and bulldoze it!' Her words jumped on top of each other.

Carlos held up a hand.

'Please, from the beginning,' he said.

Lucy took a deep breath and, at a more measured pace, repeated everything Nigel had said. Well, almost everything – she couldn't bring herself to explain that she'd lost Nina's key. The other news was bad enough without adding that, she told herself.

Rahel was pensive. 'I think you are right, Lucy, about this scarred Nigel. Remember when the Bull Commander dropped his mobile phone after the tiger attacked him, and Nigel's name was in the address book? Well, Aunt Larissa made it her business to find out about him. Nigel Adams is the Bulls' main contact in Australia. According to our spies, he buys thousands of footballs and carpets from the Bulls who run the jungle jails, and ships them to Australia. Together, he and the Commander and the generals are getting rich, very rich.'

'Rich enough to win an election,' said Lucy despondently, remembering that huge sign on top of Nigel's car.

Suddenly it all felt too much. Part of Lucy wished the Tiger-cat had never reappeared and the tunnel had never yawned open again. She felt as though she faced battles in two worlds – to save the Mermaid House from Nigel Scar-Skull's bulldozer *and* stop him becoming Mayor *and* stop him selling slave footballs – *and* the small matter of getting Angel safely home to her grandparents through a foreign city crawling with enemy soldiers. Knowing Angel, she would try to make them haul that rug along too. And Lucy had a headache from being thumped with a mango. She decided to run away before things got even crazier.

'Hey, we'd better get home,' she said. 'We can talk more in the morning and decide what to do. Have you guys got enough food?'

'We have enough supplies for today,' said Rahel proudly.

'Well, we'll bring some more in the morning. Come on, Janella and Ricardo. Mum will be wondering where we are. And no, you can't take the monkey, Ricardo. I think Mum might notice you've got a new friend for the Easter holidays! ' "Nice monkey, sweetie, where did you get it?" '

Over Ricardo's protests, Lucy said an abrupt goodbye and dragged him, minus monkey, out of the cubby into the tunnel. Janella was full of questions Lucy didn't feel like answering. She was over it. But, reaching the fork, she could not resist a quick sniff. Was that tantalising scent water?

12

Nigel in the News

Mum was just about to leave for work at the hospital when the kids got home, but as they said goodbye to her on the verandah there was an unexpected delay. A hot-pink-and-yellow van, covered in painted daisies and bearing the sign 'Kurrawong Flower Power', pulled up. A man jumped out with the biggest bunch of flowers Lucy had ever seen.

'Are you Lucy?' he called cheerily. Stunned, Lucy could only nod. He strode up and presented her with a glorious bouquet of deep orange trumpet-shaped lilies with black flecks deep in their throats, wrapped in black tissue paper.

'Congratulations!' he said and jogged away, stopping only to stroke a ginger cat that had materialised, purring, at the gate. Lucy saw the Tiger-cat out of the corner of her eye but was preoccupied by the note tied with orange ribbon to the flowers – and its familiar spidery hand-writing.

Dear Lucia,

Angel needs you more than ever. She must be returned to her grandparents in Telares City as soon as possible — and the carpet she was weaving must go with her. I must ask you also to unlock the dragon chest you have been guarding for me and deliver its contents, in the strictest secrecy, to Angel's grandparents.

Please don't believe anything my nephew says about me and, whatever you do, don't tell him that I have contacted you. My life depends on it. And please — keep both keys and the rug pattern safe. They must not fall into the wrong hands — especially not Nigel's. A world is at stake.

Eat this note immediately!

All my best wishes,
Nina Hawthorne

Lucy looked up – directly into her mother's eyes.

'So, does your boyfriend have a name?'

'I haven't got a—' Lucy retorted hotly – but then had no idea what to say. She scrunched the note and steeled herself to follow Nina's dietary advice, but just then the Kurrawong bus pulled up at the gate and Mum went to meet Grandma. Phew! Lucy was stoked Nina was alive, but not so keen on eating the good news. And it wasn't all good news. Nina wanted her to open the dragon chest –

and to do that, she was going to have to get the key back from stupid Nigel.

Mum drove off in the farting Mazda and soon Grandma was engaged in the serious business of slicing her marble cake, feeding T-Tongue twenty-five dog biscuits, and grilling the kids about how much they had eaten that day. Lucy had zero appetite. She glanced at the newspaper Grandma had just pulled from her bag – and her day suddenly got a whole lot worse.

Twenty minutes later Grandma had her feet up in the lounge room and was immersed in an old Errol Flynn movie with lots of sword-fighting – and the kids were holding an urgent conference in Lucy's bedroom. Nina's flowers had pride of place on Lucy's bedside table and the crinkled note and today's newspaper were spread out on the tiger rug. Nigel Scar-Skull grinned ghoulishly up at them from the front page.

ADAMS IN THE LEAD, the headline blared. Nigel's horrible stretchy smile, lips pulled back tightly to show off all his teeth, took up most of the page. To Lucy, it was a snarl. In smaller letters, another headline said, 'Candidate Says Red Tape Must Go'. What did that mean? She read aloud:

Prominent real-estate agent and importer Nigel Adams will be Kurrawong's next Lord Mayor, according to an independent poll released yesterday. The Stanley poll shows a slim majority of Kurrawong voters support Mr Adams' campaign to cut red tape and fast-track development on the escarpment. If the survey translates into votes, Mr Adams will scrape over the line in next week's election, just ahead of Escarpment Protection Coalition candidate Rosa Panckhurst. Mr Adams' controversial push to bulldoze hectares of rainforest for high-rise apartments has deeply divided the community. 'I'm delighted so many Kurrawong residents support my sensible stance on bringing wealth and progress to the city,' Mr Adams told the *Kurrawong Crier* yesterday.

Full story, page 3.

'What does it mean?' Janella asked, worried.

'They think he's going to win the election. And he wants to bulldoze the escarpment!'

'All of it?'

'I dunno. Let's read the rest.'

Mr Adams has lodged a Development Application for a large tract of his family's land, high on the escarpment. He plans to clear 20 hectares of rainforest to build 300 luxury apartments. His intends to demolish an eccentric 1940s home built for his aunt, Mrs Nina Hawthorne, who is presumed dead after disappearing two weeks ago. Mr Adams is the sole heir to the Hawthorne estate.

'My aunt's fate is a tragic mystery,' an emotional Mr Adams told the *Crier* yesterday. 'At the end, she was no longer herself. It is horrifying to see someone you love lose her mind. But she would have approved of my plans. My aunt was not one to stand in the way of progress and would want as many people as possible to enjoy her land.'

'My only wish is for this sad final chapter in dear Aunt Nina's life to be resolved with some dignity. An old lady in her condition could not have survived all this time alone. But I must face the painful truth. I have decided to hold a memorial service for my aunt this Friday if her body has not been found.'

'She's not dead!' Lucy assured the others for the tenth time, trying to smooth Nina's crumpled letter. 'But she won't let me tell Nigel that.'

Lucy wanted nothing more than to shout from the top of the roof that Nigel was a big liar and Nina was alive and anyone with a bulldozer aimed at the Mermaid House had better just go and drive it into a big ditch right now – but she couldn't. It was very frustrating.

She kept reading. 'Oh, you're joking! Listen to this!'

Mr Adams is a generous sponsor of junior soccer in Kurrawong and has recently extended a helping hand overseas.

'My business activities in East Burchimo gave me the chance to help the poorest children embrace the wonderful international game of soccer.'

Janella looked confused, and Lucy had to explain how the Bulls had even stolen the name of Telares and changed it to East Burchimo.

'If everyone played soccer I believe the world would be a better place. My company, Ten Star Imports Pty Ltd, lets East Burchimo's children become involved – and provides affordable soccer balls to children everywhere, especially here in Kurrawong,' he told the *Crier*.

'How can they believe this stuff?' squealed Lucy. 'They don't know anything about him.'

'Let's google him,' said Janella calmly, and Lucy's face lit up. Janella might not be able to find her way in the dark, but she had good ideas. Lucy grabbed Dad's old laptop and typed Nigel's name into the search engine. About 150 Nigels with the same surname came up, so she added the name of his company from the newspaper, Ten Star Imports Pty Ltd.

Bingo! He had a website. A telltale image dominated the home page: a huge white pentagon with a blue elephant inside a circle of ten golden stars.

'See,' Lucy said, grabbing her own soccer ball to show Janella. 'See, this is one of the balls Rahel and the others were making.' Looking at the emblem on the ball, a perfect match for the one on Nigel's website, gave Lucy the creeps. So did Nigel Scar-Skull's snarly smile, which also took up plenty of room on the home page, along with a slogan telling everyone to vote for him next weekend. Lucy made herself read everything carefully. It looked as though the *Crier* had just pasted its information straight from his web page! It had all that stuff about helping the children of East Burchimo become involved in soccer and how Nigel wanted the world to be a better place. Lucy wanted to spew.

Under the link 'Contact us', Lucy found a phone number and an address, down in the older part of town – 112 Harbour Road, East Kurrawong. She knew where that was! It was the road leading down to the old harbour and jetty, where Dad took her fishing. It used to be really busy, but now all the warehouses were empty, apart from a few daggy second-hand clothes and furniture shops. Only desperado bargain-hunters or fishing nuts like Dad ever ventured that far from the mall.

Suddenly, Lucy got goosebumps.

'Hey, that must be where Nigel is hiding the key to Nina's dragon chest,' she said excitedly. 'He said it was in his safe. I bet it's there!'

'But you've got the key,' Ricardo said, confused. 'Nina gave it to you in the Christmas holidays.'

There was a long silence.

'Umm – there's something I've been meaning to tell you.'

13
Planning

When Lucy had recovered from the humiliation of having to admit to her little brother that she had lost something just a teensy bit important, she managed to steer the topic back to just what they might be able to do about it. Of course, she had no idea how to break into a safe, but she did have one distinct advantage: the area where Nigel had his office was her territory.

Lucy loved the old harbour. She loved wading out under the jetty at low tide to scrape limpets and cunjevoi off the piers for bait. On a clear day, from her vantage point at the furthest reach of the jetty, she could spy black-cloaked stingrays swooping and hunting, which never failed to give her a shock of fear and pleasure. And you could catch fish, lots of them – and when the fish weren't biting, she and Dad used to explore the abandoned warehouses near the jetty. They were huge, and there was always a way to get in. Now, if Nigel's was one of them . . .

Janella scribbled down Nigel's address from the screen,

and Lucy fired up the search engine again. There was one more entry about Ten Star Imports but it did not link to Nigel's home page. It opened at a page with dodgy graphics and way too much writing. Lucy was about to click out of it when two words caught her eye: 'Kid Watch'.

She sat up straight. 'Janella, look at this. Ricardo, get over here.'

Something in her voice had the required effect. Ricardo stopped raiding the remains of the marble cake and came over.

Kid Watch is a non-profit organisation keeping the world informed about cruelty to children.
Latest news: allegations of child labour in East Burchimo.

Breathless, Lucy clicked on the link. It took forever to load.

Kid Watch has recently received reports from several human rights groups about the Pacific Island of East Burchimo, formerly known as Telares. Kid Watch is investigating complaints that the Burchimo army, which invaded Telares several years ago, has instituted a comprehensive regime of child labour. According to the Telares Welfare Association's spokeswoman, Larissa Toledo, thousands of children are held in jungle jails throughout the island and forced to work long hours making soccer balls and carpets.
There are concerns that an Australian company,

Ten Star Imports, is a key distributor of these products. Its managing director, Nigel Adams, was unavailable for comment yesterday.

'Isn't Larissa the name of Rahel's auntie?' Janella asked.

'Sure is,' said Lucy with a glow of pride. Whoa! Larissa had been busy. And now someone else out there knew what was going on. Lucy felt an enormous sense of relief.

'We've got to tell the others.'

But Grandma, who had fallen asleep on the lounge, woke up and wanted them to clean the bathroom. And the kitchen. And their bedrooms. By the time all that was over it was almost dinner time and way too late, Grandma said, to go out. Despite Lucy's best intentions, she slept the whole night through.

They finally got away the next morning, armed with about fifty of Grandma's sandwiches and some leftover marble cake. Lucy was so eager to tell the others at least some of her news that she forgot to bring a torch for Janella and streaked ahead without her. Then she remembered and had to run back.

'Sorry. I'm so used to doing this on my own.'

'That's OK, but I think it's time we got me a torch, or I met one of those bats you told me about.'

'No you don't,' said Lucy, shuddering. 'They're gross.'

'So's stumbling along in the dark. If I touched a bat and it gave me bat senses I could keep up.'

At the cubby, Ricardo's monkey loped up sideways with shrill cries of welcome and Lucy had to stop Ricardo feeding it half the sandwiches. Toro had more sense – he gobbled his down in no time, ignoring the increasingly plaintive gestures and shrieks of his monkey friend.

Lucy read the note and bits of the newspaper out loud while everyone ate. When she got to the part about Nigel holding a memorial service for Nina, she got outraged all over again.

'And she's not even dead!' she cried. 'He's burying her alive!'

'He can't bury her if he doesn't have a body,' Carlos pointed out, reasonably enough.

'You know what I mean,' Lucy cried hotly. 'He's going to bury her the day before he wins the election. It all sucks! And we don't have time to make it not suck! And Nina won't let me say anything!'

Lucy flopped onto the lounge. What she really wanted to do was punch something or someone. A few months ago she might have punched Ricardo, but she was over that now. There was always the lounge, though. Lucy gave it a good thump, choked on ten years worth of dust and had to retreat to the door until she stopped coughing.

'This Nigel, he is clever,' Rahel said thoughtfully, between bites of marble cake. 'He believes everyone will feel sorry for him because of his dead aunt, who he misses so much, then everyone will vote for him.'

There was an angry exclamation from Carlos, whose head was buried in yet another story about Nigel. 'The person who wrote this story knows nothing! Listen! "Mr Adams is a prominent businessman who has helped the poor Pacific island of East Burchimo develop export industries and improve the living standards of its people." Improve the living standards of the Bulls, they mean! East Burchimo! I cannot bear to hear that false name!'

Lucy could almost see steam coming out of Carlos' ears. Then Angel surprised everyone by trotting over to Carlos, grabbing the front page of the paper and ripping it in half! Nigel Scar-Skull's head lay in two pieces on the floor. Angel had the same look on her face Lucy remembered from last summer when she had set those little stick Bull soldiers on fire. She was definitely one weird kid – no way was she an average four-year-old. She had also inspired the monkeys, who each grabbed one half of Nigel Scar-Skull's face and began tearing the paper into little pieces.

'Don't let them rip up the other pages. We might need them,' Lucy said.

Carlos held the paper out of reach and kept reading out loud. When he got to the bit about Nigel helping kids in East Burchimo get involved in soccer, there was general outcry – which the monkeys enthusiastically supported. When it died down, Carlos spoke through gritted teeth. 'Don't worry. I promise you, we will find a way to stop this bald Bull collaborator. Without him, the Bulls cannot sell their Ten Star Jumbos and their carpets.'

That reminded Lucy to tell everyone abut the Kid Watch website. It was a good move. Carlos stopped frowning and Rahel became very excited when she realised Larissa's name was on the Internet.

Just quietly, Lucy was surprised that Rahel even knew what the Internet was. They hadn't exactly been online at the jungle jail. But all the kids seemed to know. Carlos saw straight through Lucy. 'We are not so backward, you know,' he said, cocking his head to one side and grinning slyly. Lucy blushed, and his grin grew broader.

'Yeah, OK, but, how?'

'Before the Bulls came, most people had computers.'

'Ponytail Zombie?'

It was Carlos' turn to redden as everyone laughed.

'Well, not Ponytail Zombie, but many in Telares City. Unfortunately, Ponytail Zombie believes computers have little devils inside that make them work. Larissa tried to show him how to use her laptop, but he ran away.'

'Larissa's got a laptop?'

Rahel jumped in before Carlos could answer, unable to contain her pride in her aunt. 'The rebels raided a Bull warehouse and found many computers and mobile phones and generators. Now we have a communications centre hidden in the mountains. The leaders say it is important to stay in touch with the world. That must be how Larissa is communicating with these Kid Watch people.'

The Internet at the rebel base?

'Why didn't you tell me. I could have been emailing you this whole time!' Lucy said heatedly.

'No!' Carlos returned with equal force. 'We must be very careful in case the Bulls track our communications. Our phones are satellite phones, and the Bulls could pin down our exact location if we are not careful, and bomb us. They can probably read our emails, so everything must be in code. Only a very few rebels are allowed to use the computers.'

'And Larissa is one of them,' said Rahel, beaming.

Lucy was silent, considering the implications, but Ricardo cut to the chase. 'So, does that mean you can't play computer games?'

'Yes!' said Toro, disgust etched in his tone. 'Larissa does not think it is important.'

Ricardo shook his head. Adults, they were all the same.

Rahel did not join in the general eye-rolling that followed this demonstration of the boys' priorities. She was frowning. 'Please, everyone, we must *concentrate*. I suggest our first step is to write a letter to this *Kurrawong Crier*. Before the Bulls came, my father wrote many such letters to *The Telares Times* and always they were published.'

'I know,' Lucy said enthusiastically. 'Grandma does too. She loves it. She keeps getting into big fights at Bingo about some of the things she says. She loves that, too.'

Then her momentary excitement leached away. 'But I don't think the *Crier* will print a letter from a kid,' she said, despondent.

'That is why we will not tell them,' Rahel said gently. 'Lucy, this must be your task. You must put everything you know about Nigel in the letter, but make it sound as though your grandmama has written it.'

'I can't pretend Grandma has written it! That's forgery. She'd read it and never bake us marble cake again.'

'That would be bad,' said a nervous Ricardo.

'I'll make up a name,' said Lucy, suddenly enjoying herself.

'And I will help you write it,' said Carlos in an ominous tone. Rahel looked sideways at him, opened her mouth to speak but changed her mind.

'I will assist too,' said Pablo, excited. 'We will all prepare this letter, Lucy will post it and then we will ride the River of Souls to Telares City!'

There was a collective gasp. Everyone else had temporarily overlooked that little task.

'I am not sure if we can go with you,' Lucy said slowly, indicating Janella and Ricardo. 'I don't know how we can disappear from home for so long. Everyone went crazy last time. We'll be grounded for the rest of childhood!'

Lucy felt a little hand in hers and looked down into Angel's black eyes. They held hers with a shocking intensity. Lucy's heart accelerated and she began to shake and grow hot, even in the tomb-like air of the cubby.

'No!' Lucy cried, dropping Angel's hand like a firebrand. 'I've had enough video clips.'

But she couldn't control her own memory: the vision of Angel with pretty curls, in a glorious party dress, being torn from her mother's arms. And her mother's plea to Lucy: 'She is yours now, you must look after her until you find . . .'

Lucy squared her shoulders and turned to Rahel. 'Where's that note from her mum, the one with the address of where we have to take her? Her grandparents' house.'

Rahel produced a familiar shape from her pocket. Every eye in the cubby, including those of the monkeys, was bent on that little matchbox. The gentle scrape as Rahel's long fingers slid it open seemed unnaturally loud. Then she placed a scrap of paper carefully in Lucy's right palm – as Angel's little hand slipped gently into her left and held on tight.

14
Children of Letters

It was so easy to write a letter to the newspaper . . . not!

If Lucy had included everyone's suggestions, it would have read something like this:

Dear newspaper guy,
Your story about Nigel Scar-Skull was way crap because he is a pig dog and bald. (from Ricardo)

He collaborates with the evil occupiers and the bloodthirsty justice of the righteous will fall on him for his crimes against small children who are eager to play soccer themselves. (Carlos)

I will send our monkeys to eat his ears due to the Bulls imprisoning myself and my sister in a bad house with very much hard work. (Toro)

And anyway, we don't like him because he has killed his auntie even though she isn't dead. Her name is Nina and she is our friend. (Ricardo)

I don't know much about all this but I think it sucks too. (Janella)

Mr Adams is a crucial link in a global chain of oppression that enslaves children while the generals grow wealthy. (Rahel)

And we hope he wets himself. (Ricardo and Toro)

Yours sincerely, and victory to the Tigers. (Pablo)
PS Don't write crap stories any more. (everyone)

Even Angel got in on the act, scrawling her name (with Carlos' help) on the wrinkled brown-paper bag Lucy was scribbling ideas on.

'I'm not sure our message has been communicated clearly,' Rahel said thoughtfully, after the laughter had subsided. Everyone began arguing loudly. The monkeys loved it, and set up a terrific shrieking. Lucy caught Janella and Rahel's eyes and nodded towards the door. No one noticed them grab a candle and slip out. Carlos and Pablo were still arguing when the three girls returned eight minutes later.

'*Listen!*' Rahel commanded. 'We have tried to remember the many letters our relatives have written in the past. My father said if you have something derogatory to say about someone, you must be able to prove it or the newspaper will not print it. He said if you know something is true but you cannot prove it, then the best thing is a list of questions. Lucy will demonstrate!'

Lucy took a deep breath.

Dear editor,
Do you believe in slavery?

What if children in East Burchimo were slaves?

What if they made soccer balls and carpets?

Has anyone asked Mr Nigel Adams who makes his famous Ten Star Jumbo soccer balls?

How would you feel if your country was invaded and all the children put in jail?

Yours truly,

Beryl Blinkington,
North Kurrawong

PS What if Nina Hawthorne isn't really dead?

Lucy had agonised over that last bit but had decided that Nina had, technically, only told her not to tell Nigel. She hadn't said anything about not going to the newspaper. And it was only a *question*.

The girls' letter more or less ended the argument, though Carlos still wanted to throw in some bloodthirsty threats against Nigel and the Bulls in general, and Pablo didn't see why the proud history of the Telares Tigers soccer team couldn't be mentioned.

Then Ricardo had a brainwave. 'Tell the newspaper guy about that website.'

Lucy and Rahel raised their eyebrows at each other in mock surprise.

'Good thinking, little bro!'

Ricardo tried not to look too pleased as Lucy quickly scribbled, 'PPS Check out this link: www.kidwatch .com.au – it will tell you all you need to know about Nigel Scar-Skull.'

Luckily, Rahel noticed that mistake and changed his

name to 'Mr Adams'. Then Lucy, Janella and Ricardo were commanded to rush off to the Mermaid House to type it up and email it to the address printed in the paper: letters@crier.com.au

But before they could get out the door, Rahel had another idea.

'Listen. I have thought of something. When the Bulls first invaded, my papa could not write to the Telarian newspapers any more, because the Bulls burned down their offices. So, instead, he wrote many letters to newspapers all around the world. We should do the same. Is your Kurrawong a big town, Lucy?'

'Huge,' said Ricardo.

'No way,' said Lucy and Janella together.

'It's not really big. Not like Sydney, but it's big enough,' said Lucy.

'Not big enough for us,' said Carlos, jumping on Rahel's idea. 'Lucy, you must send that letter to a hundred thousand newspapers! Today!'

'Okaaaay,' said Lucy.

'Maybe not a hundred thousand,' said Janella cautiously, looking sideways at Carlos' intense face.

'You know what I mean,' he said sternly. Then he must have realised he was way too uptight. 'As many as you can, then,' he entreated, smiling at Janella.

'Whatever you say, General Carlos,' Lucy mocked, unaccountably annoyed at the way her best friend and Carlos were still grinning at each other.

If there was going to be a reaction, Rahel forestalled it. 'The other thing my papa did was speak to reporters himself. At night, he would ring reporters all around the world and ask them to write stories. He even rang Australia. I believe this is what we should be doing. Lucy, I believe you must make contact with a reporter at this *Kurrawong Crier* and tell them yourself what is happening.'

Gulp. Rahel was really fired up, but Lucy didn't know if it was a good idea to ring anyone. They would know she was just a kid and think she was making it all up. She'd been through that with her family – why would a stranger believe her? Besides, how could she prove anything?

But Rahel had support from an unexpected source.

'Carla Kowalski works at the *Crier*,' Janella said quietly. 'She's my big sister's best friend. She was school captain last year and now she's training to be a reporter. She's nice, and she's always after big stories. But all they let her write about is the Dog of the Week.'

'That's it!' said Lucy. 'Nigel can be Weirdo of the Week.'

'I'll copy the email to Carla,' said Janella eagerly. 'I know her address.'

'But,' objected Rahel, 'we need someone who writes about more than dogs. This story must appear in New York and London. It must be on television and radio!' She was frowning and beginning to get that slightly insane, extremely determined expression that Lucy remembered so well.

'Look, one step at a time,' Lucy suggested. 'They might print our letter in tomorrow's *Crier* and Nigel might be sent to jail. The Kurrawong police might arrest him before he can win the election.'

Everyone looked excited at that prospect, until Janella said, 'What for? He isn't locking up kids in Kurrawong.'

And everyone realised she was right.

'And even if they did arrest him, Telarian children will be locked up until the Bulls are defeated,' Carlos said angrily.

A heavy silence followed. Lucy cast about desperately for words that would stop Carlos scowling, Pablo looking so sad and Rahel planning something way too complicated.

'Listen, let's just see what happens with the letter. And in the meantime I've got a better idea. I'm going to break into Nigel Scar-Skull's warehouse down at the harbour and see if I can get back Nina's key. We have to unlock the dragon chest and take whatever is inside to Angel's grandparents. Who wants to come?'

'When?' Carlos and Pablo jumped up, both much more cheerful.

'Tonight.'

Only Rahel had the presence of mind to ask, 'How does Nigel have Nina's key?'

And Lucy had to go through it all over again.

15

Angel Insists

Lucy felt great as she clicked Send on the laptop and the letter zipped through cyberspace to the *Crier* and Janella's doggy reporter. It lasted until Grandma emerged from her afternoon nap and told her to hop off the Internet and help make dinner. Which gave Lucy plenty of time to worry about how they were going to spirit Angel back to Telares City without anyone noticing they were missing. And without being arrested. Or shot. Or both. And plenty of time to worry about her rash invitation to the Telarian kids to break into Nigel's warehouse. What had she been thinking? But it was too late now. The Telarians would be waiting at the pit tonight for Lucy's signal.

By the time Mum arrived home from work, tooted the horn, drove Grandma home and stumbled back up the front stairs, she was ready for bed.

'You lot should be asleep,' she accused, but she couldn't help smiling at Lucy and Ricardo bouncing up and down on the verandah, very pleased to see her. 'You've got Grandma wrapped around your little fingers. And, Janella,

I bet your parents don't let you stay up this late. Now, all of you, get to bed!'

She dragged herself into her bedroom and they heard her hippy music start. Lucy looked at Ricardo. He looked back at her. Janella just looked worried.

'Goodnight, Mum,' Lucy called out.

No answer. To be on the safe side, they all crept into the tiger-rug room and waited for her dreamy tape to stop playing. The three of them lay on the rug, stroking their favourite creatures. Ricardo chatted away to 'his' monkey as though it could answer him. Janella was fascinated by the black horse, but no matter how much she concentrated she had no strange visions. As usual, Lucy contented herself with stroking the tiger's fur, while T-Tongue curled up on the elephant.

Between Mum's music and the soft carpet, they might have drifted off to sleep, but for a disturbance at the window. The Tiger-cat was silhouetted in the moonlight, standing up on its back legs, scratching urgently at the glass. Lucy opened the window but the Tiger-cat refused to come inside, pacing back and forth on the windowsill, tail twitching, fixing each child in turn with a challenging stare. T-Tongue gave a strangled whimper and tried to climb out the window but the cat give him a gentle biff on his nose and he subsided.

'She wants us to go now,' said Lucy, but she was talking to an empty room – Ricardo was out the door and Janella, who seemed to have lost all restraint, was following. Lucy grabbed T-Tongue's lead, remembered this time to take a torch and took off, pausing for an instant outside Mum's door. No hippy music, no nothing.

Outside, everything glowed silver under the full moon. As a ginger feline shape flashed up the path beside the chook pen, Lucy felt that familiar hunting feeling rise, and she broke into a loping trot. By the time she hit the stairs, she had overtaken the others (partly because Ricardo kept leaping into the lower branches of trees) and was running full pelt. In one fluid motion, she crouched, leaped, landed on all fours, shook herself and smiled at the Telarian kids waiting in the pit in a shaft of moonlight. The Tiger-cat's purr beckoned from up ahead. Ricardo bounced down the wall after her.

'You did it again,' he called, half-accusing, half-admiring.

'And what were you doing in those trees, monkey man?' she retorted.

He grinned and held out his arms to one of the two golden monkeys Toro held.

Janella came down more slowly.

'You are on time,' said Rahel to Lucy, consulting a rather battered, old-fashioned watch with luminous hands. Curious, Lucy asked to look.

'It is my father's,' Rahel said simply. 'Larissa kept it for me. He wants me to have it until he escapes.'

Lucy didn't know what to say.

'He will, you know,' Rahel said sternly, as though she had read Lucy's mind. Lucy swallowed. How hard would it be for everyone to escape from the Bulls? Rahel and Toro's parents had been in jail for months – and they didn't have a Tiger-cat (or a tiger) to help them. Unless the rebels took back their country, a lot of people were going to stay in jail for a long time. But Lucy didn't want to say any of that. So she changed the subject.

'About the warehouse. Hardly anyone goes down to the harbour, especially not in the middle of the night,' she reassured the others (and herself). 'Dad and I sometimes go fishing there at night, but we're usually the only ones. And most of the warehouses are falling apart. I hope Nigel's is one of those. It will be so easy to get into.'

Janella looked disbelieving, but she wasn't going to be left out. Nor were any of the Telarians, even though entering Kurrawong was a huge risk. Ricardo and Toro were extremely excited, which was a bit of a problem, especially with those bright golden monkeys clinging to their necks. They wouldn't listen to their big sisters, but they did listen to Carlos, who persuaded them that their monkeys could get caught or lost if the boys didn't do exactly what they were told. He won Lucy's undying gratitude by convincing both little brothers that their important job was to hide outside the warehouse and warn the others if anyone came along.

'It is far too dangerous for Toro to go into the warehouse. If Toro got caught, the police would think he was a thief and lock him up, just as the Bull Commander locked you up, Ricardo,' Carlos said.

Ricardo looked at Toro's plastic sword.

'OK, Carlos,' he said, to Lucy's utter astonishment. She waited until he wasn't looking, then mouthed a surprised 'Thank you' to Carlos, who shrugged his shoulders and grinned.

Then Lucy remembered. 'Angel! We can't take Angel.'

But the little girl in question simply walked over to Carlos and demanded to be picked up, wordlessly stretching out her arms.

'I think she wants to come,' said Carlos.

'Angel – it might be dangerous,' Lucy pleaded. But Angel had plenty to say tonight.

'Lucy must take Angel. Lucy will take Angel. The Tiger-cat says so.'

Everyone was still shocked at Angel's vocal skills, but no one looked too surprised at the idea of the Tiger-cat insisting on anyone doing anything, except perhaps Janella. Angel buried her head stubbornly in Carlos' neck, like a baby koala. Then the Tiger-cat leaped from the pit onto the top stair and turned, tail lashing, as if to say, 'How much longer do you intend to keep me waiting?'

The hunt was on.

16

Night Adventure

As one black dog and one gang of kids clung cautiously to the shadows beside Nigel Scar-Skull's warehouse, their leader was silently and deeply relieved that the old harbour really was deserted. Even the streetlights were few and far between. They had agreed to wait ten minutes outside just to make sure no one was around, and Lucy was finding the delay excruciating. She couldn't believe she had let the Telarians come this far – it was a monumental gamble. Inviting them into the Mermaid House last summer was one thing; leading them through Kurrawong was quite another, even in the middle of the night, sticking to the quiet back alleys. The journey had been unnerving. Now there was the small matter of a break-and-enter.

Number 112, Nigel's warehouse, was the last one, closest to the water. A lonely light burned a few metres away, marking the start of the wooden jetty. Its partner at the other end answered, faintly, way out in the harbour.

When Lucy was little, she would run as fast as she could all the way to that far end of the jetty, trying not to touch the cracks between the giant old wooden beams. She'd gaze down, down, deep into the turquoise depths and imagine herself on a pirate ship, being forced to walk the plank. She always escaped of course, to run all the way back again, this time trying to step *on* the cracks. She loved watching the tugboats guide into port the great container ships, their names written huge in languages she didn't understand. Cranes unloaded mysterious crates that she imagined brimmed with a pirate's treasure from far-flung places – pearls, cinnamon and silk. But when the new harbour was dredged, everyone left, except crazy fishermen like Dad.

So why, Lucy wondered, did Nigel Scar-Skull choose such a decrepit part of town for his office? The warehouses were literally falling down, and most were home only to rats and bats. Nigel had boarded up the broken windows at the front of his and installed a solid-looking door, but even so, it was a dump.

Why not move to the new harbour, with its brand-new container terminal? That was where all the huge boats came in now. If Nigel's crappy Ten Star Jumbos were arriving in the big international freighters, he would have to truck them from the new harbour all the way over here. It didn't make sense.

'Time's up,' hissed Rahel, consulting her watch, which had been hurriedly adjusted to Kurrawong time.

Lucy took a deep breath. 'This way.' With T-Tongue at her heels, she slid cautiously along the side of the warehouse. It seemed to take forever. Finally, her questing hand found the corner of the building and she peered around into bright moonlight. Last time she had explored down here, all the back windows had been broken and she had simply climbed in. She was hoping nothing had changed.

Nothing had. Big old windows gaped like wounds and shattered glass lay everywhere. Lucy turned back to check that everyone wore shoes. They all did, except T-Tongue. She picked him up and he licked her neck, but managed not to make a sound, even though she could feel every muscle quivering with excitement under his thick fur.

She peeked again. Nothing moved, but there were no shadows to hide in. Lucy signalled 'Hurry' and slipped around the corner, clinging to the side of the building. The moon was a glaring spotlight. She dashed to the closest window, checking quickly for shards of broken glass that could cut hands and feet. Lucy listened carefully for a few seconds, dropped T-Tongue through the opening and told him 'Stay'. Then she sprang easily up onto the frame and dropped down to join him in the cavernous darkness.

One by one, the others followed, Lucy holding Angel while Carlos climbed in. They huddled nervously in the darkness, suddenly unsure, now they had come this far, what exactly to do. Carlos broke the impasse.

'Ricardo and Toro will stay here close to the window and warn us if anyone comes,' he hissed. 'And Angel must stay with them.'

Lucy shone the torch in Ricardo's face.

'Got that?'

'I already said OK!' he said, wounded.

But Angel refused to be put down, refusing even to return to Carlos. She clung to Lucy, impersonating the monkeys clinging to the boys' necks.

'It's not fair if she goes,' Ricardo began, way too loudly, but Carlos silenced him with a big-brotherly hand on his shoulder.

'Your job is important,' he whispered, and Ricardo subsided. 'You two must crow like a rooster if anyone comes. No, shriek like a monkey.'

Toro and Ricardo grinned appreciatively at each other.

Everyone listened, shivering, for a few more seconds, until Lucy decided it was safe to play her torch around the room. They were in a huge room, with enormous beams, beribboned with dusty cobwebs, overhead. It smelt damp and a bit icky, just as Lucy remembered, and there were great piles of rusting machinery in the corners and fat ropes hanging from the ceiling. Except . . . what was that? Lucy stepped closer and her torch bounced off a white expanse at the far end: two walls had been built across one corner of the warehouse, sealing off a private space. Piles of leftover timber and builders' scraps were stacked nearby.

'There,' whispered Lucy. 'That must be Nigel's stuff, behind those new walls.'

Crossing the open space was excruciating. Her feet felt clumsy and loud. She forced herself to concentrate and let that cat-like feeling awake, until she was padding quietly along one of the walls, T-Tongue at her heels. There were no windows or doors, not on this side at least, but when she slid around the corner and the torchlight bounced off a glass-topped door, she snapped the torch out. What if someone was working back late? They could have seen the flash.

The others had moved up just as quietly, and stood listening. Nothing stirred and there was no light inside.

After a minute Lucy stepped closer, grasped the door handle and turned. Locked.

Pablo grabbed her torch and darted back into the darkness towards the old machinery. At the clash of metal on metal, everyone flinched, then again at the sound of something heavy being dragged across the floor.

'What's he doing?' squeaked Janella.

'I don't know, but get ready to run, just in case,' Lucy breathed. She tuned every sense to high alert. The torch bobbed closer and Pablo was back, carrying something long and heavy. Lucy grabbed the torch from him and shone it on a businesslike piece of metal. Pablo looked very pleased with himself. He whispered, 'Just shine the torch on the lock for me, then turn it off.'

With shaking hands, Lucy obeyed. Pablo forced his makeshift tool into the gap between door and frame. Wood splintered, shockingly loud in the echoing warehouse. As the sound died away, Lucy's heartbeats seemed to fill the room. Surely someone had heard! She listened with every cell of her body, but all was quiet.

The door swung free and Lucy knew what she had to do. She stepped inside and stretched out her bat sense. She could feel objects along each wall, but could not tell what they were. She stepped further inside to make room for the others crowding behind.

Suddenly Lucy was overwhelmed with the desire to lie on the ground. She handed Angel to Carlos and this time the little girl did not resist. Lucy sank to the floor and then, next to her, Rahel was doing the same. Lucy's snake sense stirred like a sleepy muscle, then slithered into life. All at once, her skin was alive to the slightest vibration in the floor. She knew exactly where each of the others stood, breathing raggedly, poised to run at the first sign of danger. Her snake mind quested ahead but nothing stirred in Nigel's lair. She licked her lips, tasting the air. Then her cat nose took over, sniffing great gulps of information. But all she smelled was fresh sawdust, paint and something leathery.

Rahel's quiet words echoed her thoughts.

'I believe it is safe,' she said, close to Lucy's ear.

Lucy clicked on the torch, and caught Janella looking oddly from her to Rahel as they climbed to their feet. Carlos and Pablo were still sniffing the air, noses wrinkled, faces taut with concentration. She said a silent thanks to the Tiger-cat for the skills given to them all. Emboldened, she encouraged Janella, 'Tell me what you can smell.'

Janella looked at her strangely but gave it a try. Lucy almost laughed out loud at her surprised expression.

'Everything stinks!' Janella hissed.

'It's because you have been with the Tiger-cat. Soon you'll walk like a cat,' Lucy whispered back jubilantly. Her triumph was short-lived. As she turned to run her torch around the room, she gasped in horror.

17

Holding Hands

Lucy saw hundreds and hundreds of Ten Star Jumbo balls stacked in crates, taking up an entire wall of Nigel's office. Piled nearby was roll after roll of carpet.

Lucy marched over. Carlos was hot on her heels, held up only by Angel, who was struggling to be free of his arms, her urgency unmistakable. He let her down and the little girl ran to the nearest rug and tried to drag it from the stack. It was way too big for her and her little fingers could not get a grip. Lucy gave her the torch to hold instead, and all the teenagers helped unfurl the rug.

They were silent as Angel played the torch over the pattern. It was a crude rendering of the tiger rug, with a tiger, bat, elephant, snake and monkey, but woven coarsely, without the silky gleam and gorgeous colours of the real thing; a rough sketch, compared to the one Lucy adored. And, as though the designer had run out of ideas, the same five animals were repeated again and again.

Suddenly Angel dropped the torch. When Pablo retrieved it, Lucy was horrified to see Angel trembling violently, kneeling on the rug, palms pressed flat against the pile.

'Angel, what's wrong?'

When Angel turned, her eyes held such a forceful expression that Lucy took an involuntary step backwards. She shivered and her head began to spin. Reeling, she could see . . .

the children who had woven the carpet, chained just as Angel had been, but they weren't in the jungle jail – they were in a huge room, a warehouse. Lucy's hands flew to her own throat, where a collar and chain bit deep

– and the spell was broken.

Carlos stepped up and touched her shoulder gently.

'Did Angel show you something?'

'Yes.' Lucy's voice was small. 'More kids. The ones who made this carpet, I think.'

Carlos placed his hands on the rug. 'I feel nothing,' he said after a moment, frowning.

Impulsively, Lucy reached out and clasped one of his hands, pressing her other palm flat against the rug. Carlos looked at her strangely but did not resist.

'Try again,' she urged.

Placing his other hand on the rug, he closed his eyes and Lucy concentrated with him. Instantly, like a blow, she felt the bite of a collar. The tremor in her mind, body and heart leaped across whatever divided her from Carlos. She felt his answering shudder and then she was lost in a sea of dreadful images. Only Carlos' strong grip saved her from drowning in loneliness – but then his grasp tightened painfully and she couldn't prevent a cry of pain.

'Carlos!'

He dropped her hand as though it burned, but not before Lucy had breathed in his anger and grief and longing for his parents, and choked on his sharp fear of being taken prisoner again. With her next ragged breath, she understood his rage and thwarted desire to protect the children who had made these rugs. She knew his thoughts, because they were hers too.

Then it was Carlos' turn to reach for her hand again and say with awkward kindness, 'I did not mean to hurt you. Come, there is nothing we can do for them tonight.'

Hot tears welled in Lucy's eyes and then she remembered they had an audience. Caught in the spotlight of Pablo's torch, Carlos again let go of her hand, as if he'd just realised he was holding it. Janella, despite the crease of anxiety on her forehead, gave Lucy a tiny sideways smile. Oh great!

Head on one side, Rahel looked from Carlos to Lucy and back again, but if she had any questions about her friends' strange behaviour they would have to wait: she was in business mode. She gestured to Pablo to shine the torch so she could examine the fake tiger rug more closely.

'A poor copy,' she said witheringly and strode to the wall, where she began methodically counting the soccer balls that were stacked right up to the ceiling.

'. . . ninety-eight, ninety-nine, a hundred. OK, a hundred in each crate and there must be . . .'

'Fifty crates,' called Carlos, from the furthest pile. He had paced down the length of the wall, counting by touch alone.

'That's five thousand balls,' Rahel calculated, a bitter note in her voice. She turned to the rugs, counting the closest pile.

'Fifty in each pile, times twenty piles, makes one thousand carpets,' she announced, her voice calm and businesslike again. 'We must find out how much this Nigel is selling them for.'

Again, she didn't give anyone time to answer, directing Pablo to shine the torch around the office. Its beam picked out a desk, a couple of filing cabinets and a large, imposing safe. It was an old-fashioned model, straight out of one of Grandma's movies, but there was nothing old-fashioned about the tiny red light that Lucy saw burning low down on the wall to the left. The hairs on the back of her neck stood up. She looked to her right and sure enough there was another light at exactly the same height on the opposite wall.

'Don't,' was all she could say as Angel lunged towards the safe, but the little girl was too quick. She knelt before it, both hands pressed against the combination lock.

'It's alarmed!' Lucy hissed. The older kids jolted, as if a collective electric shock had passed through them, but Angel remained glued to the lock, shoulders hunched in concentration. High above the safe, a red light began to flash.

'I think she's set it off already,' Lucy warned. 'Dad told me about them. It's like a laser. When you walk between those two lights on the walls, you break the signal and an alarm goes off.'

'Excellent,' Carlos said heavily.

But the little girl relaxed her hunched shoulders and began to giggle, hands still resting on the lock.

'Angel,' remonstrated Lucy, 'it's not funny. We have to go.'

'NO!' Angel said stridently.

'Shhhh!' Mass personal jinx.

But the little girl giggled again and held out her hand to Lucy.

Lucy strode over, ready to grab the little brat and run, but the second she touched Angel's hand she cried out. Then she was swirling, speechless, into another reality.

When Lucy shuddered back into her own skin thirty seconds later, Angel was grinning like a cat and did not resist when Carlos swept her up in his arms. Rahel grabbed Lucy's hands.

'Lucy, move! We have to get out of here,' she said brusquely.

But it was Lucy's turn to be stubborn. She shook her head urgently.

'I know the combination,' she whispered. 'I don't know how, but Angel beamed Nigel into my head. It was like I was him for a few seconds, standing here, unlocking the safe. Yuck!' Lucy's hand flew up to check she still had hair.

'So, what is it then?' asking Rahel calmly, taking the torch and shining it on the lock.

Lucy dropped to her knees.

'Nine, three.' The lock spun smoothly. 'Seven, four and . . .', there was an audible click, '. . . and nine again.' Holding her breath, Lucy swung the heavy handle. With a clunk, the door opened. Rahel's torch revealed a familiar shape and Lucy reached inside, breathless, grabbed the clear plastic ziplock bag that held the key and pocketed it. But her hand was drawn back to a pile of white envelopes, and on an impulse she grabbed the fattest one and shoved it in the waistband of her jeans.

'Let's get out of here. That alarm went off ages ago!'

'But I cannot hear anything,' said Pablo hopefully.

'That's because it's probably going off in the police station!' Lucy hissed.

At the mention of the word 'police', Rahel killed the torch and everyone streamed through the busted door, relying only on cat's eyes and bat senses. They were remarkably quiet for kids in such a hurry, and Lucy noticed that Janella moved just as stealthily as anyone else. But, reaching the window, she heard several things in quick succession: the squeal of brakes as a car pulled up out the front, and two roosters crowing. Or was that two cars, one rooster, and a monkey?

Lucy swung Angel over the sill. Someone dropped T-Tongue out and the puppy landed on his feet, turning loyally to wait for Lucy. In the moonlight, she could see the panic on the Telarian kids' faces as they scrambled out after her. They were in a strange place, in a foreign land, with an unknown enemy on their tail. It was up to her to get them out of this mess.

'This way,' she hissed, and loped off to her right towards the next warehouse. She slipped into a pool of shadows, the others crushing in behind her, just as pounding feet rounded the back corner of Nigel's warehouse. No time to stop. She knew where she was – kind of. If they could just get past the next two warehouses, there was a dark alley connected to a web of back lanes that led, if you knew what you were doing, all the way to the city. Lucy was confident they could lose any pursuer once they reached the alley.

Her cat feet flew and soon she sprang into the dark mouth of the alley. The others were right on her heels and Lucy saw the smaller shadows that were Ricardo and Toro with a huge sense of relief. It didn't last. As a shout went up from the warehouse, Lucy heard her own voice ask, 'Where's Angel?'

18
Catastrophe in Kurrawong

There was a collective hiss of fear as everyone looked down to knee-level, where Angel should be. Lucy grabbed the torch from Rahel and shone it into the shadows to see if the little girl was hiding, but all she saw was T-Tongue's bloody footprints, a trail leading right to where they stood.

'T-Tongue has cut his paw,' she said. 'And Angel . . . must be back there.'

Her stricken expression was echoed in every other face. His mouth a grim slash, Carlos turned and slipped out of the alley, back towards the warehouse. Rahel and Pablo followed. Lucy turned to Janella.

'I'll take them,' Janella said before Lucy could open her mouth. 'See you back home.' Turning to Ricardo and Toro, she flashed a blinding smile Lucy would be forever grateful for. 'C'mon, you two. Let's feed your monkeys!'

Lucy had the distinct impression both boys wanted to split themselves in two – but the mention of their simian soulmates and Janella's charm did the trick, and they bounded after her.

The whole exchange had taken only seconds. Lucy was alone in the alley, except for T-Tongue, who held one paw in the air as though it hurt but still looked eager for action, ears pricked. Lucy felt in her pockets. Good, a hanky. She shone the torch briefly on the puppy's cut and was relieved to see it had stopped bleeding. She quickly bandaged his paw and clicked out the torch again as another shout went up from the warehouse.

She found Rahel, Carlos and Pablo lurking in the last pool of darkness, watching intently. Her heart sank. There, in the blinding moonlight, stood Angel with a burly security guard leaning over her, his hands on her shoulders.

'Who are you?' he asked, not unkindly, but Angel collapsed and lay still. Lucy lurched forwards in the same instant as Carlos, every instinct demanding she rush to Angel's side. Rahel and Pablo's urgent hands restrained them.

The guard dropped to one knee. 'Hey!' he exclaimed, as two more guards rounded the corner from the road, carrying long baton-like torches. 'She's fainted. We'd better get an ambulance.'

Carlos moved faster than thought, picking up a rock and hurling it, not at the guards, but in the other direction, towards a huge pile of discarded bottles and drink cans. Bullseye! It triggered a dreadful clattering avalanche, as though an army of intruders was scuttling away.

'Over there! They're getting away!' Carlos' ruse had worked brilliantly. The two new guards gave chase, dodging rolling bottles and cans, leaping the remainder of the pile of rubbish and disappearing into a shadowy maze of abandoned offices behind the warehouse.

'Search everywhere,' the first guard shouted after them.

Another guard ran up and leaned over Angel. 'Boss!' he exclaimed. 'There is something I must tell you!' But his leader was impatient. 'Later!' he snapped. 'Go back and search the warehouse. Check nothing has been taken. I'll get the police.'

His subordinate ran to the broken window and climbed in, his torch making crazy shadows. Lucy heard the crackle of static as the leader reached for his two-way radio, then the call sign: 'Unit One to base, Unit One to base, come in, please.' Waiting for a reply, he stooped to examine something on the ground. Lucy froze: T-Tongue's footprints! The guard's head jerked up, following the trail until he seemed to gaze directly into the shadows where the kids stood like stone. Then he reached out to Angel's limp form and shook her shoulder roughly.

In that instant, Lucy understood two things: there would never be a better time to act, and it would take more than Rahel and Pablo to hold her back. Eyes locked on the guard, she felt the blood simmer in her feet, drawing heat from the earth itself.

'Unit One to base, Unit One to base, urgent, urgent!' The guard turned his back and began to walk towards the smashed window. 'Unit One to Unit Two, I need you here, over.'

Crouching, every muscle and sense locked on her uniformed prey, Lucy crept forward. She made a stealthy rush, feeling the air part like silk before her. Though she made no sound, some intuition must have alerted the guard. He swung to face her, eyes widening in shock, but it was too late – he froze, his radio slipping uselessly to the ground from petrified fingers. One part of Lucy heard the crackle of static and understood the disembodied voice calling: 'Base to Unit One. What have you got? Over,' but the ancient boiling in her blood had no use for words, no use for anything but the inexorable roar her body could no longer contain.

She leaped for the guard's throat. He fell heavily, head striking the concrete, and then she was upon him, one paw on his chest, jaws ready to rip his heart out.

Whoa! The part of Lucy that was still Lucy reared backwards and stumbled away from the unconscious guard. A low growl to her left made every hair on her body stand up. Stalking from the shadows was a Telarian tiger, eyes burning blood-orange in the moonlight. No – not moonlight, torchlight . . .

'Boss. I am thinking you must come to see this. The door to the office, it is . . . Boss! Mother of God!'

Lucy swung her head to the right and met the eyes of the guard sent to search the warehouse. His frantic gaze switched between Lucy and the huge tiger. In that split instant, Lucy recognised him. But it couldn't be! And then, with a blood-curdling scream, he was gone, fleeing back through the window into the bowels of the warehouse, as the tiger sprang after him.

Suddenly Carlos was at Lucy's side, gathering Angel's limp body in his arms. Rahel grabbed Lucy's hand and dragged her back into the shadows, where Pablo stood holding a frantic T-Tongue's collar. They sprinted for the alley, just as the other pair of guards stumbled back over the pile of cans and bottles and raced towards their fallen leader – only to freeze mid-stride as, from the warehouse, there came a terrible scream.

19

'Angel Won't!'

Ten anxious faces – seven human, two simian, one canine – surrounded Angel as she slept in the cubby. She was pale but her breathing seemed normal. She had woken once, looked at Lucy, lifted her arms mutely and snuggled in, burying her plaits in Lucy's neck.

Everyone was shaken and almost too tired to talk. What was there to say? They had Nina's key, but the adventure had gone horribly wrong. The adrenalin that had flooded Lucy's body during the emergency had subsided in exhausted despair. She slumped onto the lounge with Angel, barely registering Carlos' worried glance. Suddenly, she remembered holding his hand and the intensity of sharing his emotions. She felt her face flush and closed her eyes, glad of the shadows.

But darkness brought a rush of images: children in collars; running from the guards; Angel collapsing; a Telarian tiger in *Kurrawong* – and, most intense, the predatory wave of energy that had engulfed Lucy when she attacked the security guard.

He had touched Angel – and Lucy had wanted to tear his throat out and eat his heart. That really shook her. The guard was only doing his job. Dave Williams at school, his dad was a security guard. Lucy hoped the man she'd attacked wasn't Mr Williams – and, whoever he was, she hoped he wasn't badly hurt. The same went for the guard who had screamed in the ware— Oh no! Lucy snapped out of her depressed reverie and sat up straight. She had to tell the awful news but it was going to be hard to get a word in, as an argument was suddenly raging between Rahel and Pablo.

'We must go back and destroy all the balls and carpets,' said Pablo.

'That is irrational,' snapped Rahel.

'We must,' he insisted.

'Pay attention, Pablo! Angel was almost lost to us tonight. And what, pray tell, happened to your mission of returning her to Telares City? Until this evening, you refused to speak of anything else.'

'Of course I know we must return Angel, but I also know we cannot let these monsters profit from their crimes,' Pablo insisted stubbornly.

Lucy was surprised to see Rahel lose her cool.

'You are being foolish and rash,' she shouted. 'What good will it do if one of us is detained and incarcerated again? It won't stop the Bulls keeping children prisoner. They have slaves all over the island!'

'But we cannot allow this bald Bull collaborator to make profit from his crimes. It is unthinkable! We must set fire to the carpets and balls!'

Seeing Rahel speechless, Lucy seized her chance.

'I think Pablo is right,' she said. 'We have to stop Nigel somehow.' Rahel's face fell and Lucy quickly added, 'But Rahel is also right – we can't risk going back. The place will be crawling with guards from now on. Besides, at least two of them got a really good look at me and – this is bad – one of them recognised Angel.'

There was a stunned silence, before everyone began clamouring.

'Shut up!' Lucy shouted. 'Listen, that second guard, the one the tiger chased, he was in the Telarian militia – he worked at the jungle jail with Ponytail Zombie, I swear. And that means he knows who Angel is. He would take her back to a jungle jail.'

Angel made an urgent sound in her throat and everyone went quiet, gazing at her with a mixture of hope and fear. Her eyes opened, then her mouth opened and closed, then a tiny sound emerged.

'Angel won't . . .'

No one dared to breathe. In a bigger voice, Angel repeated, 'Angel won't . . .'

'What won't you do?' asked Carlos gently.

'Angel won't go back,' the little girl whispered. 'Angel will go to her grandmama and grandpapa. Angel won't go back to bad men.'

'No,' the others said in chorus, 'Angel won't go back.'

'And we will take you to your grandmama,' said Lucy.

'And Angel's carpet will come too.' The little girl sounded very certain.

'And Angel's carpet will come too.' Lucy didn't sound quite so certain, but it was the only thing she could say, even if she had no idea how she was going to complete either task. Satisfied, Angel conked out in her arms, asleep again immediately.

'How are we going to get to Telares City?' asked Lucy after a long minute's silence, looking at the others despairingly. 'We can't be away from home for that long. We'll be missed. And after last time, Mum, Dad and Grandma will really go psycho!'

A quiet voice took her by surprise.

'It's OK, Lucy,' said Janella. 'I've thought of a plan.'

Lucy turned, bemused, to find her friend smiling, as though congratulating herself on a brilliant idea.

'We'll just ask if we can camp up at the clearing you told me about,' Janella said blithely. 'It's not bushfire season, so they'll let us.'

Pablo, eyes gleaming, leaned forward.

'And you will not need to be away for long. Perhaps not even a day. I know this river and I know the caverns. I spent much time there with my parents when they were working. It was like my playground. I had my own small boat and I explored everywhere. All we must do is row across the river. People are coming and going from there all the time and we will just blend in. I believe it will be quicker than trying to reach the harbour. There are many stairs cut into the rock on the other side of the river, leading up into the streets of Telares City. Once we are in the city it will be very easy to walk to Angel's grandparents' house.'

Suddenly, Lucy could not stop yawning. Ricardo was nodding off in the corner, cuddling his monkey. Perhaps Lucy was asleep too? The very idea of going back into Telares, let alone crossing a strange river to a strange city crawling with Bull soldiers, seemed like a crazy dream. But, looking at Angel, she knew she couldn't dodge the mission, no matter how much she wanted to.

'OK. Tomorrow it is. But right now I'd better get Ricardo home,' she said, yawning again, 'or Mum won't let us out the front door for a week.'

Lucy passed Angel to Carlos and persuaded a reluctant Ricardo to disentangle himself from his soulmate. After saying their goodbyes, the Kurrawong kids trudged up the tunnel, to find the Tiger-cat awaiting them in the pit. She escorted them all the way to the bedroom and curled up on Lucy's bed, relegating T-Tongue to the tiger rug. It was only when Lucy got undressed that she remembered the envelope from Nigel's safe. Truly shaken by the night's events, she had no energy to think about it, let alone open it. She shoved it under her mattress and was asleep in three seconds.

20

The Easter Bunny

Lucy awoke to bright sunlight and a brighter mother.

'Happy Easter, everyone! Rise and shine!'

Lucy groaned, barely able to keep her eyes open. Then her mother's words sank in and she sat bolt upright. Easter Sunday! How had she forgotten? There was a massive Easter bunny at the end of her bed and one for Janella too. Janella's parents were away in Melbourne for the whole break, but Mum wasn't going to let her feel left out. Ricardo stumbled in, rubbing his eyes, clutching a half-mutilated chocolate bunny. He immediately keeled over on the rug as though he was about to fall asleep again.

'Come on, Ricardo, I can't believe you're too sleepy to finish your bunny. That would be a first. I'm the one who should be sleepy, after the day I had at work yesterday. You kids had an early night, didn't you?'

'Yes, Mum,' said Lucy dutifully, stifling a yawn. Well, they did have an early night, or rather, an early morning. Her stomach lurched at the memory of last night's events.

Mum frowned. 'You don't look very happy, Lucy. Actually, none of you do. What's wrong? It's Easter! Cheer up!'

'It's cool, Mum, I was just having a bad dream when you woke me up,' Lucy said quickly.

'It's OK, Mrs Ferrero,' said Janella, 'I'm just missing Mum and Dad a bit. It's my first Easter away from them.'

'And I just want a monkey,' chipped in Ricardo, 'a real one!'

'You'll have to settle for an Easter bunny,' said Mum, but the awkward moment was broken.

'Mrs Ferrero, would it be OK if we camped up in the bush tonight?' Janella asked, out of the blue. 'I love camping and Mum and Dad are always too busy.'

Lucy shot her mother a nervous look, but she was glad Janella had taken the initiative.

'I suppose that would be OK,' said Mum. 'It's not bushfire season any more. But nothing risky. And be careful near that waterfall.'

'Yes, Mrs Ferrero.'

'Mum, do you want us to make a special Easter breakfast?' asked Lucy quickly. Of course she did, so the kids got busy, preparing boiled eggs and toast, pancakes and maple syrup and coffee. The world began to look a whole lot better – until Mum turned on the radio.

Turning to local news, Kurrawong police have urged people not to panic despite reports of tigers running wild in the old harbour area. A security guard investigating a break-in at a warehouse says a tiger knocked him to the ground. He was treated in Kurrawong Hospital for minor head injuries. Police say there is no evidence to support the man's story, and suggest he slipped, hit his head and was knocked unconscious and may have been hallucinating. However, another guard claimed he saw two tigers: one crouched over his injured workmate and another which chased him into a warehouse. He is under sedation. Two more guards at the scene claim to have seen at least one tiger. However, police say no Australian zoo has reported any tigers missing. Meanwhile, a child, apparently part of a juvenile gang, was detained at the scene, but escaped. Police say they are more concerned about the juveniles who broke into the warehouse than about any reports of tigers.

Luckily, Mum totally misinterpreted the stunned silence that descended on their festive breakfast. 'Oh, don't look so worried,' she laughed. 'Tigers in Kurrawong? As if. The police don't even believe those guys. They were probably drunk, like almost everyone else who ends up in Casualty on Easter Saturday night. You watch, I'm going to hear some crazy stories at work today.'

'But you can't go to work – it's Easter!' exclaimed Janella, clearly desperate to change the subject.

Lucy's mum smiled. 'Do you think people don't get sick at Easter? There are car accidents, people drink too much, sometimes they even eat too much! Oh yes, and they get chased by tigers. Not! Anyway, you watch, my ward will be full.'

Then came words Lucy would rather not have heard. 'Speaking of injuries, what happened to T-Tongue's paw?'

There was a stricken silence, while everyone stared at T-Tongue's bandage, and then Lucy decided to tell the truth. 'He walked on broken glass and I wrapped it up in my hanky.'

'Let me have a look,' said Mum. T-Tongue brought the examination to a quick end by the simple expedient of licking her nose. 'I guess you're OK,' said Mum, 'but we'd better pick up that broken glass. Do you know where it is?'

'Yes,' said Lucy truthfully, hoping against hope that Mum would stop asking questions. 'I'll look after it.'

The doorbell saved her.

'Good girl. That will be Grandma, probably with fifty Easter eggs. I'll need your help, girls, or Ricardo will eat them all at once. I don't want him arriving at work in an ambulance!'

When you counted all the tiny ones, Grandma really did have fifty chocolate eggs. Strangely, none of the kids showed much desire to eat them – even Ricardo secreted most of his in the pockets of his pants.

'I tell you, that boy's getting sick,' said Grandma, frowning. 'He's off his food!'

'Not as sick as he would be if he ate them,' said Mum, exasperated. 'Besides, the kids are all spending the night up in the clearing. They might need an Easter egg or twenty around the campfire.'

'Are you sure that's a good idea, after what happened last time?' asked Grandma in a huff. She and Mum were still arguing half an hour later. But finally, the kids got the go-ahead – and the key to the room with all the camping gear in it. Bummer. They were going to have to make this trip look real, and that meant hauling a whole lot of stuff they had no intention of using up the hill.

'What was all that on the radio about *two* tigers?' asked Janella, staggering under the burden of a completely useless tent when they were out of earshot of the house.

'You only mentioned one, and I wasn't quite sure I believed you about that!'

'Well, I only saw one, and that was weird enough,' said Lucy, puffing under her load of a cast-iron camp oven, a hammock and about seventy of Grandma's sandwiches.

'You know, sometimes I think . . .' She trailed off and Janella had to prompt her.

'C'mon, what do you think?'

Lucy stopped walking.

'Well, it's as if I summon the tiger.' She glanced sharply at Janella, afraid she would laugh, but her friend had stopped, frowning in concentration.

'Go on.'

'Well, every time the tiger has shown up in Telares, I've really needed it to. I've been really scared or angry, like when the Bull Commander almost broke Rahel's arm. Or when I saw the kids at the jungle jail in real life for the first time. A tiger attacked the guards that time as well, and gave Ricardo and me the chance to run away . . .'

The words 'real life' prompted another memory. 'And in my psycho dreams, before I even went to Telares, a tiger always showed up when I was scared and angry. I dreamed about Rahel and Toro before I met them. I was angry because Toro was so little and hungry and the guards were horrible – and I dreamed a tiger helped them escape. When I met Rahel, she said that that was exactly what happened. A tiger attacked and they ran away while everyone else was freaking out.'

Janella silently considered her friend's words. Lucy ploughed on.

'But last night . . . was different. It was as if . . . I *was* the

108

tiger. I can't explain it and I'm not sure I like it. I had to stop myself tearing that security guard's throat out. It was as if I could taste his blood and . . . I wanted to. I really wanted to.'

Lucy's eyes stung. 'And then, on the radio, when they said there were two tigers, I just freaked, I really freaked.' She looked desperately at her best friend. 'I don't know what to do, Janella. Sometimes I feel out of control, and I don't know what's happening. And we almost got Angel arrested, and now I've dragged you into all this. But I don't think I can stop. I didn't tell you what it felt like last night when I held Angel's hand and she showed me the kids who had made that carpet.'

'You didn't tell me what it felt like when you were holding Carlos' hand, either,' said Janella, laughing for the first time.

Lucy blushed and kicked her friend gently on the shin. 'It wasn't like that, but I'll tell you if you want.'

'Oh, I want,' said Janella, clearly pleased to have something to tease Lucy with, something to break her dark mood.

'Angel let me see the kids who made that carpet and feel what it was like for them. I was the one wearing a collar and chain. Then, when I held Carlos' hand, he could as well. But it was more than that: I knew exactly what he was feeling. He acts all tough, but I know how scared he is of getting caught again and how much he misses his parents and how angry he is about them being murdered.'

Janella went pale and still. 'I can't imagine that,' she said after a while.

More walking, less talking, Lucy decided.

At the steps, Janella paused. 'We have to help them, don't we?'

It wasn't really a question, but Lucy answered anyway. 'I reckon.'

21

Teaching Tiger

The dragon chest was still hidden in the shadows near the entrance of the tunnel where Lucy had left it last summer. Trembling a little, Lucy fitted the distinctive filigree key they had risked everything to get back into the lock. It opened with a clunk. That wonderful scent of sandalwood wafted up, and there was the leather pouch and the envelope that held the precious pattern. Janella oohed and aahed over the tiny box inside the pouch, with its jewelled tiger. The box rattled gently and Lucy opened it to reveal the other key, its delicate design exactly the same as the one now safely back around her neck.

'We think this is the key to another dragon chest in Telares,' she explained. 'The Bull Commander stole the chest from the jungle jail when the Bulls first took over, but he couldn't open it. We think that is why he got so excited when he saw Nina's key around my neck. He thought it was the key to the chest.'

Lucy closed the tiny box and put everything carefully in her backpack. Only then did she remember the envelope under her mattress. Oh well, it was too late to go back and get it now. Telares awaited.

Back at the cubby, Angel was much better, giggling when she saw Lucy and lifting her arms to be picked up. Ricardo's monkey did the same, but his giggle was more of a shriek.

'We've brought the stuff and we've got until lunchtime tomorrow,' Lucy said. Turning to Pablo, she asked, 'Do you think we can get there and back in time?'

'I am not familiar, of course, with this new tunnel, but the journey across the river and through Telares City should not take too long – if nothing goes wrong,' he said.

Everyone went quiet, contemplating one or two things that could go wrong. Ricardo demonstrated his usual short attention span. 'We were on the radio!' he blurted out, delighted. The Telarians went from worried to horrified, even Toro, who usually got excited just because Ricardo or one of the monkeys did.

'What do you mean?' asked Carlos suspiciously.

Lucy took a deep breath, wishing she didn't have to tell them.

Afterwards, there was a heavy silence, then Rahel said the last thing Lucy expected. 'Oh well.'

'Oh well!' Carlos retorted sarcastically, but he never got to launch into a furious speech because someone much smaller beat him to the punch.

'Tiger Lucy,' Angel said, shocking everyone into silence, and not just because no one was used yet to her speaking at all. Angel pointed at Lucy. 'Tiger Lucy,' she repeated.

Lucy's throat grew so tight she couldn't have spoken, even if her jelly brain had come up with something to say.

Janella took one look at her stricken face and spoke for her. 'On the radio, they said the guards saw two tigers, not one, and now Lucy is freaked out – like *totally*!'

Angel giggled. It sounded really creepy in the shadowy cubby. Rahel cocked her head and considered Lucy, who stood with arms folded and shoulders hunched. 'What is it that you are *totally* afraid of?' she inquired calmly.

Lucy shook her head dumbly. Rahel turned to Carlos. 'Last night, you were closest to Lucy. How many tigers did you see?'

Carlos looked up suddenly and held Lucy's gaze. Silence stretched taut as a drum. 'I saw two. Just for an instant, when you leaped at the guard, Lucy, I swear I saw a tiger flying through the air. Except I know it was you. You sprang, but a tiger landed! It reared over him and I thought it was about to kill him. But then everything went blurry and I couldn't see properly for a few seconds – and then you were back, looking as if you had seen a ghost! Then another tiger came from the other direction and I picked up Angel and ran.'

'Why didn't you report this last night?' asked Rahel, an accusing note in her voice.

'Because I thought I was going crazy.' Carlos voice was low.

'Try being me,' said Lucy heavily, and crumpled onto the lounge. 'What is happening?' She turned to Rahel, as though she should have an answer. Rahel did not reply immediately, which gave Angel time to repeat 'Tiger Lucy' and giggle again in an extremely irritating way.

'Shut up!' The words were out before Lucy could stop them. Everyone except Angel shot her an accusing look, but the little girl just stepped closer to Lucy and took her hand. She said, without a trace of a giggle and with an instant, mysterious maturity, 'Lucy, you are tiger girl.'

There was a long silence.

Then from the shadows came Ricardo's derisive 'Yeah, right!', and Carlos added, 'From this moment, the person formerly known as Lucy will be known as Flying Tiger Girl.'

And everyone cracked up.

Maybe the tension of the night before had finally got to them, but no one could stop laughing. The monkeys loved it, screeching and cavorting about with the boys. T-Tongue barked excitedly and the Tiger-cat leaped up on the table, tail lashing, to get away from this profoundly undignified behaviour.

Finally, Lucy wiped away tears of laughter. 'I don't know, maybe I am Tiger Girl. Something weird sure is happening, and I can't seem to help it. So, maybe we'd better use it. Has this ever happened to anyone else?'

Rahel nodded slowly. 'Remember when the Bull Commander stamped on my wrist and T-Tongue attacked him?'

As if Lucy could forget! Last summer, when Ricardo and the other little kids were locked up in the jungle jail, the Bull Commander had caught Rahel and Lucy trying to break them out. He had almost broken Rahel's arm – which made T-Tongue really mad. Still only a puppy, he had attacked – and so had Rahel, despite her pain. She had leaped at the Bull Commander's head, just like the Tiger-cat in a really bad mood. But the Bull Commander had wrestled her down, and aimed his heavy boot at her body.

That was when Lucy totally lost it – or found it, depending on your point of view. She would never forget the protective rage that had boiled up from the earth into her chest, and was unleashed in a silent wave of power that seemed to petrify the Bull Commander. By the time she roared out loud, it was too late for him – a real tiger had sprung from the jungle.

'Of course I remember,' she breathed.

'Well, the Bull Commander hurt my arm so much I couldn't see at first. Then all I could see was him – and I was filled with rage. I remember jumping for his head, and I wanted to tear his eyes out with my claws.'

Lucy almost missed it.

'With my claws,' Rahel repeated intently.

Lucy's eyes widened.

'Yes, for a minute there I felt like the Tiger-cat. I had teeth and claws and . . .', she paused, '. . . no mercy.' Rahel looked down, and when she spoke again her voice was tinged with shame. 'But the Bull Commander was stronger than me. If it had not been for you, Lucy, he would have kicked me unconscious.'

'You mean, if not for the tiger,' said Lucy.

'No!' Rahel flashed. 'I saw you paralyse him with your eyes before the tiger attacked. I understand fully this phenomenon, as I have studied the lives of tigers. They begin their roar at a frequency that their prey cannot hear – at first. They fix them with their eyes and begin their silent roar and the animal is quelled and frozen with horror. It knows what is coming but cannot escape. The silent roar is the most dangerous – by the time it can be heard, it is too late.'

Lucy shivered. Rahel's words rang true. It explained how she had cowed Blake on the bus just by looking at him with her tiger eyes and threatening him with her tiger heart. 'This is too much,' she said, more to herself than anyone else.

'No,' said Rahel. 'For me it is not enough!' She wore that set, determined expression that usually meant she was about to abandon her characteristic calm and go psycho. She faced Lucy squarely. 'I want what you have.'

'No, you don't,' Lucy burst out. 'I almost killed that guy last night. Then they would be hunting a murderer, not just a bunch of kids. And he wasn't doing anything wrong. He was just doing his job. We were the ones breaking the law. I don't care about the militiaman, he's working for the Bulls, but the security guard is different. He could have kids at my school for all I know.' Lucy was angry to feel tears scratching. 'I know I don't want to kill anyone, but when Angel fainted, I just, I just . . .'

Carlos nodded in violent agreement.

'But,' Rahel continued softly, 'we don't all have your . . . tigerish skills. And we can't all call tigers to our sides.'

'That's what I've been thinking too,' Lucy whispered.

The laughter of a few minutes ago seemed to have occurred in a different century.

Pablo jumped up on the table, startling everyone.

'There is a very simple solution,' he announced grandly. 'Today we embark on a dangerous mission to return Angel to Telares City. But first Lucy must teach us to be tigers!'

Carlos snorted, but Rahel, with an admiring glance at Pablo, who now seemed a little uncomfortable up on the table, said, 'That is exactly my conclusion.'

Lucy's conclusion was 'Oh great!' But she kept that to herself, because something else was bugging her: how did Angel know Lucy had become a tiger at the warehouse? She had been unconscious! But it was pointless trying to work it out, and the urging of the others could not be resisted. They all agreed there was no time like the tigerish present.

22

Carlos' Ordeal

First, Lucy made everyone stand in a circle and hold hands.

'Someone make me mad,' she demanded. Everyone looked at Ricardo.

'What?' Mr Innocence exclaimed. That was enough. Tuning in to her own mood, Lucy realised all she had to do was *look* at her little brother to feel a tigerish irritation stir. It began in one big toe, just a twinge, but if she focused she could feel it course into the arch of her foot. At Carlos' urging, Ricardo poked his tongue out at her – and the twinge twisted around her kneecap and shot up her thigh. 'It's working!' she cried. 'But only in one leg.'

'We need something that makes you really mad,' said Janella.

'Girls can't play soccer,' said Carlos, straight-faced, and Lucy felt a distinct twinge in her other leg, her goal-kicking leg.

'We've got a competition up in the rebel base – you can come and watch if you like,' Carlos continued pleasantly.

Lucy's goal-kicking leg began to throb furiously, but Rahel's cry distracted her.

'I am experiencing a hot and tingly sensation in my feet – and I very much want to kick Carlos!'

'Excellent,' said Lucy.

At that, Carlos' right leg jerked involuntarily, as if an invisible doctor had whacked his knee with a rubber hammer to check his reflexes. He turned red. Lucy had the distinct impression that if Pablo and Janella weren't gripping his hands his kick could have connected, but whether with her shins or Rahel's, she wasn't sure. She grinned sweetly. 'Getting the idea?' Another involuntary kick and Carlos growled a grudging 'Yes!'

Angel giggled in that slightly disturbing fashion she had adopted recently. Toro and Ricardo, eyes closed, concentrated fiercely. Watching them, the older kids struggled not to laugh.

'I'm not getting angry. It's not fair!' an outraged, red-faced Ricardo shouted after a minute. He opened his eyes at a combined burst of laughter, glaring at each teenager. 'It's not fun—' he started to say, but his own involuntary karate kick intervened. He appeared amazed as his right leg flew out from under him, aimed squarely at Lucy's head. Janella, holding tightly to his right hand, hauled him back before he could make contact and he landed on his bum. That did it; everyone fell to the floor giggling.

'OK,' spluttered Carlos. 'I think we are getting it.'

When they had recovered enough to get serious about their training, Carlos insisted on going first. Glowering, he stood rigid, eyes closed, flanked by a troubled Lucy and an even more troubled Rahel. He had only been practising

119

being angry, as he called it, for about fifteen seconds, and already the girls who knew him best were wondering if this was a good idea. Carlos held Lucy's hand with Chinese-burn strength. On his other side, Rahel was grimacing in pain. The others completed the circle.

'You have to hold the roar in your chest, Carlos,' Lucy ventured.

'Shut up!' he returned in a throaty growl, and Lucy and Rahel exchanged another worried glance.

This could get ugly, Lucy realised, but even as she tried to form words of warning, his frown grew heavier and she began to tingle. Then, swift as thought, Carlos' anger engulfed her. She struggled to remember her own advice as her chest boiled and a mighty roar threatened to bring the roof down. Images flashed before her and, dimly, she heard Janella cry out.

The Bull Commander! At his feet, on a concrete floor, a woman lies in a pool of blood, her long dark hair fanned out, her neck at a sickening angle. Beside her lies a tall, strong man, but his body is curled like a baby's and he does not move.

'No!' A cry of pure heartbreak fills the room and the Bull Commander turns, a gloating smile on his ruined face.

Lucy struggled to return to her skin but an awful keening had replaced the roaring in her chest. Despair dragged at every limb, sucking her down to oblivion, to be buried in mud and rock. For endless seconds she plummeted, a dark star called back to the beginning of time . . .

'No!' From somewhere, Lucy found strength to resist. Pure anger charged through her stony limbs and for an instant she was incandescent, a flaring sun at its moment of birth, exploding up and out from dragging nothingness in a furious decision to live.

Gasping, Lucy found herself back in the cubby. Someone was moaning. 'Carlos!' But his hand slipped from hers and he collapsed, eyes rolling back in his head, all colour drained from his face.

'What happened?' cried Rahel, desperately feeling for his pulse.

'I don't know. It was too big, too much. Is he breathing?'

'Just,' said Rahel, and burst into tears. Lucy felt her own eyes smarting and quickly got a grip. One of them had to stay calm, but she was used to it being Rahel. 'Carlos!' she called again, and gently stroked his dark hair. 'It's OK, you can come back now. It's over, Carlos. We're not practising angry any more.'

Carlos muttered something unintelligible but he did not open his eyes. Angel wriggled between Lucy and Carlos, and insisted, 'Carlos must open eyes! Carlos will open eyes!'

He stirred again, and Angel pinched his cheeks hard. 'Wake up!' she insisted, like a petulant toddler.

With another groan of protest he opened his eyes to see Angel's face about a centimetre from his own. 'Angel,' he pleaded, 'leave me alone!' But the little girl had no mercy, pinching him again. 'Ow!' he cried with more feeling. 'Yes, yes, I'll get up.'

Angel sat back, beaming with satisfaction. 'Carlos awake,' she said triumphantly.

'Sit him up,' Lucy squeaked. Pablo propped Carlos up with cushions and Janella offered him a cup of water. For a long moment he didn't say anything, but just sat on the cold earth floor, pale and shivering, swallowing tiny sips. He couldn't hold the cup and Janella had to keep bringing it to his lips.

'He's in shock,' said Lucy, belatedly remembering first aid. 'We have to get him warm.' Together, the teenagers got him upright and helped him totter to the lounge, where they wrapped him in blankets.

'I am in excellent health,' he tried to reassure them. 'Thanks!'

Rahel shook her head. She had regained her composure, but the dusty track marks of tears remained. 'It is dangerous, what we are doing,' she whispered to no one in particular, then reached for Carlos' hand.

'I thought you might die,' Lucy said, and this time, had no embarrassment about taking his other hand, feeling terribly guilty about where her tiger-training class had taken him.

'I wanted to die,' he said softly. 'The Bull Commander, it was like a movie, he showed me how he murdered my parents.'

Then Lucy's tough Telarian friend lost it. He buried his head in the blankets until the sobs passed and, with a ragged breath, looked up to find his friends red-eyed in sympathy.

'You know, I have not cried since my parents were . . . were murdered. Not once in the jungle jail, not once at the rebel base, not once in a whole year.'

'Tell us what just happened,' said Lucy.

'I liked being angry. I was hunting the Bull Commander. I was going to kill him. It built and built like an earthquake till I thought the roof would cave in. I hunted the Bull Commander through my memory and I could have eaten him! But then I found him and – whamm! I was back in the Bull jail in Telares City and he *stole my anger*. He stole it and used it against me. He enjoyed showing me what he did to my parents, he liked what it did to me. And that's when I felt myself dying. And I didn't care any more.'

'I know,' breathed Lucy and, looking about at the others, she knew they did too.

'We must be more careful,' Carlos said, with more strength. 'I'm telling you, the Bull Commander was inside my mind. And the rebel spies are correct – he is filled with determination to catch us. All of us. I could feel it. He will never forgive us for humiliating him. I always thought his strongest weapon was his gun, but now . . . I am not so sure. I think he has other . . . talents.'

Carlos' voice trailed off and then he looked at each of his friends in turn and said quietly, 'I think you saved my life. I had nothing left, and then I felt your fire, I felt you all there. You were telling me not to die.'

The thought of the Bull Commander inside Carlos' mind gave Lucy chills. How had he done that? Or was it just Carlos' nightmare? Had the Commander's gruesome contact with the Telarian tiger given him talents, the way the Tiger-cat and the other creatures had given them to Lucy? She didn't know what to think.

'One thing is for sure,' she said, frowning. 'We have to learn to control this tiger training. If getting angry can take you where Carlos just went, we're going to have to get good at it, learn how to protect ourselves – against who-ever we might meet in our minds.'

Rahel nodded sombrely. 'We have no choice.'

23

Raising the Roar

'I've got a plan,' Lucy announced to her somewhat dubious tiger trainees. It had taken some time, but she'd figured it out, sitting quietly in a corner of the cubby while everyone else ate a desultory lunch. By the time she'd finished chewing on her thoughts, the others had chewed all of Grandma's food – but she didn't mind. She had worked out something important. Tigers were her territory, after all. She was the one who had summoned one in the first place, had felt her very self dissolve into something raw, wild and dangerous.

Ignoring her friends' doubtful expressions, she spoke confidently. 'We're not all going to hold hands any more. We raised way too much power, much more than we could control. Instead, I'm going to work one by one with everyone. We're just going to practise raising the roar and holding it in our chests for ten seconds at a time. Then we're going to growl.'

There was a moment's silence.

'And?' asked Ricardo.

'And nothing. That's it!'

'That sucks!' he said rebelliously. 'I want to roar!'

'I mean it, Ricardo. You saw what happened with Carlos. We stop there until we know what we're doing.'

Lucy turned to the others.

'I'll work with one of you while the others stand guard. If it looks as though it's getting out of control, you all have to jump in to break it up. OK? And if anyone starts to fall, the way Carlos did, then I'll feel it and I'll break the grip straight away.'

She turned to Carlos. 'And you, you're going to stay where you are and shut up!'

She knew he was still shaken, because he didn't complain. He even smiled weakly.

'OK, who's first?' Lucy challenged.

Toro stepped forward, and Rahel frowned.

'Okaaay,' said Lucy, thoughtfully, 'I guess he has to learn some time. He might need it where we're going today.'

Rahel nodded reluctantly, but planted herself as close as she could to her little brother without actually touching him.

'But you have to put those down,' Lucy said, indicating Toro's monkey and sword. 'Now, hold my hands, and think of something that makes you mad.'

His little face grew serious.

'Not too mad!' Lucy hastily cautioned, but Toro had already become unnaturally still, and his grip on her hand tightened. Then he gasped, and made a bleat of distress. A succession of emotions chased across his face: panic, terror, desperation. Even as he stood with all his friends in the cubby, Toro fled some awful memory. Lucy felt it too, a dark emotion, as strong as a rip in the surf.

Rahel cried out, appalled. 'It's happening again! Let him go!'

But just as Lucy went to drop his hands, Ricardo yelled, 'Come on, Toro,' making everyone jump. Toro wrenched his eyes open. 'If you had our sword the Bull Commander would wet himself!' Ricardo urged.

Toro's grip became downright painful. He took a deep breath – and then Lucy felt the familiar tingling in her feet, as energy charged from the earth's bones into hers.

And then . . . Toro growled! Not a very big growl – more of an underground grumble than a jungle rumble – but still the testing growl of a cub who had surprised himself. 'I'm not scared any more,' that growl said, 'and I'm going to be big one day and you're all going to wet yourselves!'

His big sister beamed.

'Yes!' roared Ricardo and almost knocked Lucy over to high-five his shell-shocked friend.

This was way too much for the monkeys, which emerged with shrieks and much cavorting from a dark corner and wrapped themselves around the heads of two small, growling boys.

There was no stopping Ricardo after that. 'My turn!' he demanded. He had absolutely no trouble learning to growl. Turning to Toro afterwards he confided, 'I just thought about Spiderman comics.' His Telarian friend appeared confused, prompting a long and involved explanation of arachnid superheroes and the cruelty of an older sibling who threw her little brother's comics in the bath just because he had told Blake's little brother . . .

Ricardo's voice trailed off. Rahel looked at Lucy admiringly.

'What did he tell someone's little brother?'

Too late, Lucy realised the hole she was in.

'Well, ummm, it was nothing really . . .'

'I told him Carlos was Lucy's boyfriend,' said Ricardo helpfully, 'but it's not true, so it wasn't really bad.'

Even loyal Janella burst out laughing at Carlos' horrified face. Lucy felt herself blushing. Worse, both feet were instantly red-hot as the mother of all roars rose through the floor. She fought for control.

'Shut up *now*! All of you!' Lucy glared about the cubby. 'We've got work to do! Pablo, it's your turn.'

Desperately trying to look serious, Pablo stepped into the middle of the room, but catching Janella's eye was his undoing. He fell over, making the weirdest high-pitched laugh Lucy had ever heard. She stamped her foot. This was gross – like having an army of little brothers.

'*Get up!*' There was enough raw roar in her voice to make the monkeys slink into the corner.

Pablo composed himself. 'Sorry,' he said, scrambling to his feet with barely the hint of a smirk.

'So you should be,' snapped Lucy. 'We're running out of time and you're the one always going on about getting to the River of Souls.'

Lucy glared at everyone.

'OK?'

'Mum reckons meditation would be the best thing for Lucy's bad temper,' said Ricardo conversationally, to no one in particular.

Not even Lucy's roar could drown out the shrieks of

laughter that followed. It was left to Angel to clamber up onto the table, blow out all the candles and, for her surprised and suddenly blind audience, announce just three ringing words: 'River of Souls!'

24

Tigerish Tricks

The rest of the training session had its hairy moments too. Pablo didn't get very mad, but he did get sad. Lucy thought she would have to break his grip at one point when the image of his parents, locked away in a jungle jail somewhere, threatened to swamp him, but Pablo gritted his teeth and growled his resistance. Then he was rumbling quietly, a perfectly controlled mini-roar that had Lucy tingling and Rahel grinning with relief. When Lucy finally dropped his hands, Pablo blinked several times, confused, then spontaneously jumped up and down on the spot, declaring, 'I did it! I was truly tiger-growling! Let's do it again!' The monkeys were especially pleased.

Predictably, Rahel's session was a demonstration in self-discipline. She held hands with a strong, confident grip and Lucy felt a rush of memories and strong emotion, held immediately in iron check. Neither the past nor the Bull Commander would ever again control Rahel – Lucy understood that much through her fingertips. Then Rahel made a sound low in her throat and, just as Lucy felt a wild roar threatening to burst, the Telarian girl gripped even harder and trained her will to the task. Her magnificent growl, when it came, was almost a purr.

'You were great,' Lucy said afterwards. 'I thought you were going to lose it, but you held on.'

'I was truly incensed,' Rahel admitted shyly, 'but I was the mistress of my own emotions.'

'Whatever,' said Lucy happily.

Janella, a little to Lucy's surprise, proved herself a natural. Somehow Lucy had thought that her friend would struggle because she had had less contact with the Tiger-cat, but she raised a respectable roar easily, and controlled it. Lucy began to feel more confident, but when Angel sprang up, she hesitated. She had not expected that. But Angel was in no mood for delays. She took Lucy's hands in a surprisingly strong grip.

'Ready!' she piped.

Lucy, who suspected Angel already knew more tigerish tricks than she let on, pleaded with Rahel: 'Keep an eye on her!'

Rahel stepped closer. Instinctively, the others drew nearer too, forming a circle around Lucy and Angel, but careful not to touch them. Lucy took a deep breath and met Carlos' worried eyes.

'It's OK,' she said – almost certainly a lie.

He nodded, absent-mindedly stroking the glossy coat of the Tiger-cat, who was regarding Lucy with inscrutable golden eyes.

'Angel, I want you to think of something that makes you feel . . .'

There was no need. Like a red tide, a familiar image rose in her consciousness, but this time Lucy was ready.

Angel and her mama. The soldiers are close, too close. Angel clenches her tiny fist around the note from her mama. The Bull Commander shouts. A sea of brown uniforms. A soldier grabs Angel, drags her from her mother. He is strong, but not strong enough to break the line of sight, of feeling, that links Angel with Lucy.

Lucy fought for control – and won. She let a growl rise gently, warmly, through her tummy, into her chest – and held it, like a simmering kettle. One, two, three . . . nine, ten! The roar sat comfortably in her chest, a purring warning, confident in its immense, perfectly controlled power.

But she was unprepared for what happened next: a sliver of that power, sharp as a laser, burned up her spine and lit up her skull. Lucy was conscious of golden heat, but no pain. Then the light, or was it sound? – settled in the centre of her forehead, like a bright, tightly coiled snake. An impossibly pure, high, clear note of music filled her every cell. Her eyes, with that humming snake of light and sound to help, looked deep into Angel's. It seemed perfectly natural for sunlight to flood the dark water of the little girl's eyes . . . and then Lucy was diving in the golden depths of not Angel's, but the Tiger-cat's eyes, the Tiger-cat's mind . . . and the bond that joined Lucy to that mysterious feline had never felt stronger as she swam deeper and deeper into a new vision.

The slap of oars . . . the pull and drag of a little wooden boat on a mighty river. The cavern it flows through is gloomy but, far away, sunlight beckons. And waiting, where the river meets the sun, is someone who longs to see her. No, not Lucy. It is Angel their heart calls for. Lucy will take Angel home. Lucy must take Angel . . .

Lucy blinked, and gradually the sensation of light and sound subsided, slithering down her spine vertebra by vertebra. The music faded and the purring roar rolled gently back into the ground beneath her feet.

She felt new and clear, as though every cell were awake for the first time. Angel held her eyes for a long moment and, once again, Lucy was overwhelmed by the idea that the little girl was closer to a hundred years old than four. Angel giggled and the spell was broken. She wriggled free of Lucy's hands, raced back to the lounge and threw herself down next to Carlos and the Tiger-cat. Carlos had gone pale again and kept looking from Angel to the feline on his lap as though something didn't compute. The hand that had been stroking the creature was frozen in mid-air.

Lucy looked to Rahel for help and met the same incredulous expression.

'What?'

'Didn't you see?' breathed Rahel. 'Angel turned into a Tiger-cat!'

Something in Rahel's voice penetrated Lucy's euphoria. She looked closely at her friend, then turned and met a pair of innocent black eyes and an equally demure golden pair. The Tiger-cat blinked, yawned and stretched. As if seeking to avoid interrogation, it slid smoothly from a stunned Carlos' lap and loped out the open door. Lucy turned questioningly to Angel, but was rewarded only with a mysterious smile.

'Don't ask me,' Lucy said. 'The Tiger-cat never explains

anything – and neither does Angel. All I know is we're running out of time.'

They collected their things and gathered near the table. Lucy searched Janella's intense, excited face and realised her friend did not have a clue what she was getting herself into.

'Janella,' she started, then paused, searching for the right words. Rahel found them first.

'We appreciate your help, Janella,' the Telarian said gently, 'but you do not have to come with us. It may be – will be extremely risky. More dangerous than last night. I don't think you understand. The Bulls, they have no mercy . . . when the time comes to set sail on the River of Souls, we will do it knowing some of us may not return.' Her voice caught on the last word, and she turned slightly away so no one could see her face.

Lucy shivered, overcome with the memory of Rahel as she had first met her in a dream, a prisoner of the Bulls.

'It's true, Janella,' she said quietly. 'In Telares, everything is for real – especially the bad things. If I thought I could leave Ricardo behind without him following or dobbing, I would.'

'Well, I'm coming. We have to get Angel home, and we have to help all those other kids,' Janella said calmly. 'Remember?'

'I remember,' said Lucy softly, 'but I don't want to have to tear out a Bull soldier's throat to save your life.'

The night soaked up her words.

'*I* wouldn't mind,' murmured Carlos.

Only the small boys laughed, their monkeys echoing them with eerie lunacy. Lucy studied Carlos' face, once again grown hard with hurt and hate as though someone had turned out a light. Unbidden, a promise unfurled in her heart. *OK – if I have to be Tiger Girl, then I'm in charge of what happens to my body. I won't lose control again. If I have to hurt someone to save my friends I'll do it, but I'll know exactly what I'm responsible for. And I won't kill anyone, not even a Bull.*

Lucy met Angel's eyes and, even though she had not spoken her thoughts aloud, she had the distinct impression the little girl had heard every word.

25
Tunnelling

An imperious miaow sounded. The Tiger-cat, eyes glowing and tail lashing, leaped back through the door and onto the jungle jail rug lying forgotten in the corner. Angel ran to crouch beside the creature until their foreheads almost touched and a loud purring filled the cubby. No one was surprised when Angel turned to say with a determination that belied her size, 'We go now! With Angel's rug. The Tiger-cat says so!'

'Well, maybe you and the Tiger-cat would like to carry it?' suggested Lucy sweetly.

But Angel was already gone. The small boys took off after her, their golden monkeys shrieking. Reluctantly, Lucy and the other Telarians hoisted up the rug, blew out the candles and stumbled out, an unwieldy centipede. Janella followed with the torch.

Nearing the fork in the tunnel, Lucy had a moment of panic. *We don't even know where we're going*, she thought. But the torch soon flashed red on the Tiger-cat's eyes. The creature waited at the mouth of the unknown passage. It miaowed again and sprang into the darkness. *Here goes nothing*, Lucy thought, and stepped into the gloom.

Only a few paces in, any doubts about where the second tunnel led were resolved. The scent of fresh water was a magnet for Kurrawong and Telarian kids alike, tempting and tantalising their heightened senses. Janella trotted up to Lucy.

'It's working,' she hissed.

'What?'

'My nose, it's working. I can smell water and – mud.'

'Congratulations!'

Janella giggled.

'But I wish I didn't need this silly torch. You lot are so good in the dark.'

'You're telling me you want to carry this rug instead?'

Lucy and the Telarian teenagers crept in single file, the rolled-up rug on their right shoulders. It was frustratingly slow, especially as Ricardo and Toro had scampered ahead. Lucy's arm and shoulder already ached under the strain. She was aware of a steady dripping all around, gritty, crumbling sandstone walls under the questing fingertips of her free hand, and the air stale and thick with old earth. Cutting through it all was the powerful scent of fresh water, drawing them on, ever deeper into the mountain.

T-Tongue was way too excited to wait and kept rushing ahead of the boys to sniff this new world, and then back to Lucy, skittering on jubilant paws, getting under everyone's feet.

'T-Tongue!' Lucy reproved, but he totally ignored her, bounding ahead into the darkness. Then a horrified yelp showed he had caught up with the stalking Tiger-cat, who had no intention of letting a mere dog lead the way. It wasn't long before Lucy felt a contrite nose on her hand, and for the rest of the journey T-Tongue was a model puppy, heeling obediently and brushing his wet nose on Lucy's fingers every few minutes, just to let her know he was where he should be.

As the track grew steeper, Lucy's nose twitched and she felt the tiniest brush of air on her face – fresh air, blowing from what could only be the river cavern of the Tiger-cat's visions.

'Could we stop?' she asked the other rug-bearers.

She took a deep breath and stretched out all her senses. Rahel's quiet breathing behind suggested she was doing the same.

'It just gets steeper and steeper,' Rahel hissed. 'Easy for bats and cats, but dangerous for us.'

She was right. The muddy ground grew ever more treacherous. Small rivulets of water coursed underfoot and they had to concentrate hard to stay upright. Soon the party was reduced to dolly steps, staggering under the rug's weight.

'Where's Angel?' gasped Lucy, a note of panic in her voice.

'She's near me,' answered Carlos, somewhere behind.

'You OK?' she called to Janella.

'I've got a torch and no rug,' her friend said bravely, but there was a catch in her voice. Lucy was suddenly brimming with gratitude. Janella had thrown herself into the Telarian cause, Lucy's cause, without hesitation.

The wall of the tunnel become a gentle curve against her dragging fingers. Two more cautious dolly steps, and the aroma of water overwhelmed her. The rhythmic slap, slap, slap of waves kept time with Lucy's steps as, blinking, she followed the back of Pablo's head around a bend into the grey twilight of a dream . . .

The River of Souls! In the strange half-light Lucy spied slippery stairs sinking into black water. A rickety old boat, moored loosely to a rock, loomed out of the shadows to the left of the stairs. Who did it belong to?

Pablo dropped his end of the rug and clambered down over the rocks. Reaching the boat, he turned to face them and the twilight could not hide his jubilant smile.

'It is just as I remember it!' he said, much too loudly for Lucy's nerves. His excitement echoed off the rock walls.

'*Sshhh!*' Mass personal jinx.

If there were any Bulls around who hadn't heard Pablo, they would certainly have heard the others trying to shut him up. Lucy looked about anxiously but it did not do her much good. Overhead, the roof of the tunnel opened into a cavernous space, barely visible in the subterranean gloom, as though all the colour had been sucked out. She strained but the light was not strong enough for her to make out the other side of the river. A thousand Bulls could be over there and she would not know until it was too late. Wait, what was that? She squinted at pinpricks of light in the distance.

'What's that?' she whispered to Pablo, pointing.

'The lanterns?' Pablo shrugged. 'They mark the stairs up to Telares City. Look, there are many lanterns on this side of the river too.' He gestured in either direction, but Lucy had to walk down the stairs to understand. She gasped. At regular intervals, in either direction, lanterns burned in the rocky river wall.

'What are they for?'

'The ancestors,' he shrugged, as though it were a stupid question.

'Oh,' said Lucy, none the wiser.

He took pity on her.

'The candles mark the entrances to small caves. Every family in Telares City has one. When someone dies, the family cave is filled with flowers and candles, and the dead person's ashes are brought here. They are kept here for a month, with many candles burning constantly and fresh flowers every day. Then, at the end of the month, only one candle is left burning at the entrance, a little boat is built and the ashes are sent floating downstream to the sun.'

Pablo's hand traced the course of the river as it stretched away to Lucy's left – and the source of the weird grey light that filled the cavern was suddenly obvious. Wow! There was a shimmering sphere in the distance. It took a few seconds to realise it was a trick of the light: sunlight smiling through the round open mouth of the river cave! Even as she watched, the sphere pulsed brighter, light washing in ripples up the river towards her, bringing colour and definition to rocks and water, children and monkeys.

Pablo was unable to contain his glee.

'It is time!' he hissed. 'Shield your eyes!'

'I don't understand.'

'Just do it!'

Lucy was shocked into uncharacteristic obedience at

Pablo's equally uncharacteristic tone of command. She copied him and shielded her eyes with her hands, squinting towards where the river flowed to the sun. Then, with a gasp of wonder, she understood his urgency, as a blinding flash lit up the entrance to the cave.

26

Great Balls of Fire

It was as though the entire sun itself slipped through – a fiery bowling ball, rolling inexorably to the centre of the mountain and the source of that mighty underground river. Lucy's head ached and she recoiled. But light was streaming throughout the cave, revealing the immensity of the natural wonder they were standing in – a cavern like no other, arching high and wide to a roof of dripping crystalline teeth, that sparkled in the brief light.

For brief it was. It seemed only a few minutes before the blaze of the setting sun was extinguished and that strange twilight began to fall again – but not before Lucy saw how fast and wide the River of Souls ran, striving on to the sunset, as though desperate not to be left behind.

She was filled with a sense of urgency. They had better get moving. Rahel and Carlos shared her anxiety and were already dragging the rug down towards the boat. Lucy ran to help.

'Move up,' she said, exasperated, to Ricardo and Toro. The boys, with their golden monkeys clinging to them in wide-eyed awe at this strange new world, were already in the boat, sitting right in the middle. Somehow, the teenagers managed to manoeuvre the rug under the wooden seats. Carlos perched with Angel in the back, while Pablo and Rahel grabbed the oars and the Tiger-cat leaped into the prow. Only T-Tongue hesitated, running up and down on the rocky shore, whimpering, clearly unconvinced that doggies were supposed to ride on the water.

'C'mon, boy,' said Lucy encouragingly. She whistled, but T-Tongue whined all the harder. Lucy went to clamber out, but she didn't have to. The Tiger-cat fixed the enormous frightened puppy with golden eyes and gave an urgent growl, followed by a resounding purring miaow: 'Pdddr-rrrowwww!' It combined 'This will be good, there will be rabbits to chase' and 'If you don't stop acting like a rabbit yourself, we'll leave you behind.' In one almighty bound, T-Tongue landed right in the middle of the boat, rocking it dangerously from side to side – but his Tyrannosaurus tongue was clearly unimpaired.

They rowed into the strange twilight, fighting a current determined to pick up their little boat and hurl it downstream, west towards the sun. Pablo was an expert rower, but Rahel was soon out of breath and the other teenagers took it in turns to partner him. Gradually the far northern shore drew closer.

'What happens if we are seen?' Lucy asked.

'It is inevitable,' Pablo said, without breaking stroke. 'Mourners and relatives are coming and going all the time. But that is to our advantage. They will think we are a funeral party returning.' Even he didn't sound convinced and, looking about the boat, Lucy could see why. The three Kurrawong kids would be noticed immediately, not to mention the golden monkeys. And the rug was the weirdest of all. Why would anyone take a rug to a funeral and then bring it back again?

As they drew ever closer to the shore, they passed two other boats heading towards the caves, laden with flowers and black-hooded mourners carrying candles and singing sadly. Engrossed in their grief, they spared barely a glance for the children's boat.

'A few of those hoods would have been handy,' quipped Lucy, and Carlos nodded grimly. But soon their boat was bumping and grinding against a rocky wall and the time for regrets had passed.

'Let's go,' said Pablo, tying the boat to a ring at the base of a short set of stairs. The Tiger-cat and T-Tongue scampered up, with Ricardo and Toro not far behind. 'Wait!' hissed Pablo, who had clearly assumed the leadership. The boys paused, grinning as if they were going to a fun park, and Lucy glared at Ricardo. 'You promised to behave!' she mouthed.

The teenagers dragged the rug out and assumed their centipede positions, no easy task on the slippery stairs.

'I want to know why Angel wants this rug,' Lucy said grumpily, hauling her end over the top stair. 'You'd think it would just be one big bad memory.'

From the tail of the centipede came Carlos' sombre voice: 'Sometimes, it is our memories that keep us going.'

'And, if Angel and the Tiger-cat concur on this matter, it must be of some significance,' added Rahel, somewhere near the centipede's stomach.

Watching Angel and the Tiger-cat skipping freely ahead

up another flight of stairs didn't make Lucy feel any better at all.

'Well, I wish they concurred on helping us carry this significant lead weight,' she grumbled, and the others laughed, albeit breathlessly. They hauled the rug up the second flight of stairs and stopped.

'We must go over there,' panted Pablo, indicating an incline leading to a rocky platform. As they staggered upward, the forest of dripping stalactites above their heads grew closer and closer. Finally, they reached a rock wall with burning candles placed at regular intervals, marking many steep sets of stairs that led up into darkness. The centipede scuffled straight to the only one that didn't have a party of hooded mourners descending it. The boys, their golden monkeys, the Tiger-cat and Angel emerged from the shadows nearby and darted up the stairs.

And so began the gruelling climb to Telares City. Lucy's muscles burned, but she tried to focus only on her lungs. After a while, the rug-bearers all seemed to breathe as one, in rhythm with their percussive scuffling feet, as though they really were one organism with many legs. The combined sound was hypnotic and strangely, after a while, Lucy's load seemed lighter. Gradually the stairwell grew brighter and Pablo let go of the rug and ran up the last steps, squinting up into a shaft of sunlight.

'All clear,' he said and when Lucy poked her head up into the open air she had a breathtaking first glimpse of a wide, tree-lined avenue. The air was as hot as a slap in the face and smelt of wonderful food and flowers. T-Tongue was at her heels but the Tiger-cat, Angel and the boys were nowhere to be seen. She stepped out into the dazzling sun and then, without time for second thoughts, they were trudging down the street, stopping at every corner to check for Bull patrols.

Lucy's heart was pounding and Janella's face was white. They rounded a corner into a gaggle of street stalls, selling everything from flowers and live chickens to hot noodles. Lucy's mouth began to water at the smell. She spied Angel with the boys and their golden monkeys, all looking longingly at a vendor selling some kind of roast meat on skewers. Ricardo didn't appear at all worried about being in Bull territory – just hungry.

'We had a deal you wouldn't disappear,' she hissed in Ricardo's ear when the centipede caught him up. He jumped and had the grace to look ashamed, until he saw another stall selling some kind of dumpling.

Lucy couldn't believe how many stalls there were. There were even some selling carpets, and suddenly the teenagers' burden did not stand out so much. They wound their way through the crowd and Lucy was pleased to see other white faces – tourists haggling over jewellery, sitting in the shade drinking from coconuts or eating skewered satay chicken. She began to relax. This wasn't so bad. But then a tourist in a particularly loud shirt at one of the stalls met her eyes and froze, satay skewer raised to his open mouth. It couldn't be!

Nigel Scar-Skull staggered in shock. Lucy was rooted to the spot, causing the other teenagers to stumble under their load and step on each others' heels. All she could do was point. Then everything happened at once. Janella and Ricardo cried in unison 'Run!' T-Tongue barked furiously and charged as Nigel lunged towards Lucy. Nigel tripped on the puppy and skidded sideways into a stall, bringing a cage of live chickens down on his head. The stall-owner, a tiny wizened old woman, shrieked in outrage. The kids took off, dragging the carpet as best they could. Lucy saw Angel streaking ahead with the smaller boys, heading back the way they had come. Lucy looked over her shoulder and was delighted to see the old woman beating Nigel about the head with a bunch of bananas.

Her joy was short-lived. As they hurtled around a corner into the avenue leading to the river stairs, a Bull patrol came trotting towards them. Lucy almost died. Amazingly, the patrol carried on, seemingly intent on getting somewhere. Lucy panted past them, trying to press her face into the rug.

The kids were only halfway to the stairs when there was an angry shout. Lucy turned, knowing what she would see: the Bull patrol had rounded the far corner and was charging back towards them. Among the sea of brown shirts was one pink-and-orange one – and a gleaming bald head.

'Drop the rug,' shouted Lucy, and no one needed persuading. Free of their burden, the teenagers flew towards the stairs. With just a few steps to go, Lucy risked a glance back. The guards were still coming, but Nigel had stopped and was bent over the half-unrolled rug. No! They had not carried it all that way to let it fall into Nigel's hands! But the guards were gaining. Her heart hammering, Lucy skipped and tumbled down the stairs after the others and raced towards the boat, as a shouted command echoed monstrously through the cavern. In any language it meant 'Halt!' But it was the shot that cracked out, whining above

Lucy's head and splintering a stalactite into a thousand spikes, that spoke loudest of all.

Crash! Another stalactite smashed onto the stairs. The Bulls' bullets were ricocheting off the walls, sending deadly spears of stone in every direction.

'Ouch!' Lucy's yell of pain was louder than the terrified shrieks of the two golden monkeys. Running for the boat, she'd tripped on a pile of rocks that had not been there ten seconds ago and fallen heavily, whacking her head.

'Lucy!' There was more than a note of panic in Janella's voice. Turning her aching head to look for her, Lucy saw the boat riding low in the water with Angel, her little brother, Toro and the two screeching monkeys already aboard.

Carlos grabbed Lucy's hand and hauled her to her feet. They lunged for the boat as another shot rang out, and slithered aboard.

Lucy looked desperately back over her shoulder for T-Tongue as another stalactite exploded. Crash! The lantern near the boat toppled to the ground and the candle went out. With a strangled yelp, T-Tongue burst out of nowhere and leaped into the boat, claws scraping on the boards in a spectacular slide landing.

Pablo produced a knife and slashed the rope that bound them to the rock. Rahel stood up bravely and rammed a long wooden oar against the wall, forcing the little boat out into faster-flowing water. Another shot rang out and she dropped to the floor next to Lucy, losing her grip on the oar as she did so. It clunked overboard and Lucy had to grab Rahel to stop her diving in to get it.

'They'll shoot you!'

Pale as ash, Rahel nodded silently. Lucy closed her eyes in relief. When she opened them again she saw Angel curled up in Carlos' arms on the floor of the boat.

'Lucy lost Angel's rug. Lucy should look after rug! Lucy bad! Lucy will take Angel home!'

'OK, OK! I'm trying. But just don't expect to make it alive.'

The Tiger-cat was nowhere to be seen.

27

Old Man River

In seconds their little boat was flying downstream, utterly at the mercy of that ancient river. The pull of the tide was irresistible. Lucy peeked over the edge and was shocked at how quickly the stairs to Telares City were receding. She wasn't sorry, though, when she checked out the progress of the Bull patrol. The soldiers were struggling to drag a heavy wooden boat across the rocks to the river. One kept dropping the boat to fire at the escaping children, but each time the report of the rifle sounded further and further away, his bullets landing harmlessly in the water behind them.

'Does this boat have a motor?' Lucy asked Pablo hopefully.

'No,' he said, shamefaced, as though he was personally responsible for this oversight. 'But,' he said, brightening, 'neither does theirs!'

'How do you know?' Lucy and Janella asked at once.

'It is the River of Souls,' he said, as though that answered everything.

Lucy looked anxiously back at the Bulls, clearly not convinced.

'It is true,' said Rahel, smiling for the first time since they had entered the tunnel in Kurrawong. 'Telarians believe the River of Souls is where the dead start their journey to the afterlife. Motors would be an insult and are expressly forbidden. Even the Bulls have respected that tradition.'

But Lucy had stopped listening. Something had caught her eye. As their little boat swept towards the sun, the rocky walls sliding past were lit up. She gasped. The river cavern was adorned with exquisite paintings and carvings, of a size and detail she had never seen before.

'Awesome! Check this out!' she exclaimed, momentarily forgetting the Bulls had been shooting at them just minutes before.

Pablo beamed. 'It is magnificent, yes? Every year a new painting is done to honour the ancestors. We travel further and further up the river to paint and carve.'

'We?'

The pride in his voice was unmistakable. Lucy looked more closely at him. Was that a tear?

'How do you know so much?' Janella asked quietly.

'My parents, they were . . .' He paused, a catch in his voice, then took a deep breath and continued more strongly. 'My parents, they are artists. It is their task to oversee the painting and carving of the murals. I have been coming with them since I was a baby. That is why I know this river so well. They gave me a little canoe to explore in when I was just five years old.'

'Cool!' said Ricardo, who had not spoken a word since

the firing began. Then he lapsed back into uncharacteristic silence, rocking his monkey, which had finally stopped whimpering and had its head buried in his shoulder. Toro had assumed exactly the same pose. Maybe the monkeys were a good influence after all?

A spray of water in her eyes, followed by a distinct lurch of the boat, reminded Lucy that this was no art appreciation class. Their fragile boat was still flying downstream, but its passage was no longer smooth. As the mouth of the cavern loomed closer, the water was suddenly turbulent and the little boat tossed and turned. After another few metres the rocky walls suddenly narrowed, pressing closer, creating a bottleneck. The water boiled. Rapids!

In seconds, children, monkeys and one black dog were drenched as the little boat tumbled through great sprays of river water. The rocky walls rushed ominously close and Pablo stood up, armed with the remaining oar, ready to lever their craft away if he could. Lucy, clinging to the side, risked a glance overboard – and wished she hadn't. Black teeth were everywhere, ready to tear the bottom from their flimsy vessel.

'Rocks!' she shouted above the roar of the rushing water, and promptly caught a spray in her open mouth. Spluttering, she clung to whatever she could. There was nothing to be done but hang on and hope.

As the black rocks roared past and their boat escaped destruction by centimetres again and again, a strange feeling overtook Lucy. She should have been terrified, but somehow she wasn't. In fact, it was exhilarating. Looking around, she saw the same expression on everyone's faces. Pablo stood proud, feet braced apart, somehow keeping his balance unaided, oar at the ready. The others held fast as best they could, but their eyes flashed with excitement. Carlos, gripping Angel tightly, had struggled to his knees for a better look. And Angel, who could never be relied upon to have a normal kindy kid's reaction, looked positively elated. Even T-Tongue was keen, narrowing his doggy eyes against the spray.

Only the monkeys refused to look, keeping their heads buried firmly in the boys' shoulders. Lucy thought they might be whimpering, but it was hard to tell over the hiss and roar of the water.

Then the sunlight burning through the mouth of the cave dazzled her and there was no time to think any more. With an almighty roar their little boat was catapulted towards an enormous rock. Lucy closed her eyes and prayed.

28

Adrift on the River of Souls

Crack! There was nothing Pablo and his oar could do. The boat smashed once, *Crack!* and twice, *Crack!* against each wall of the cave, hurling kids and monkeys to one side of the boat and back to the other. Then, spinning, their dinghy was tossed like flotsam and jetsam into the path of the blinding sun.

Lucy cried out and shielded her eyes. Squinting, she saw the cave's open mouth was already receding. They were tumbling in the afternoon light on the widest, shiniest river she had ever seen. No longer strangled by the narrow river cavern, the water spread like a glistening bolt of silk in every direction. The current was irresistible, though, for the shore on both sides of the river was slipping by inexorably. Which was lucky, really, because to their right were the roofs and towers of what could only be Telares City and, on the river bank, a party of Bulls was launching a boat much bigger and sleeker than theirs.

That was when Lucy noticed her feet were wet – and not

just from the spray. She didn't need Janella's words of panic to understand.

'We're sinking!'

The impact of the rocks as their little dinghy was tossed from the cave had been too much for it. A crack splintered its bow, yawning wider as Lucy watched. Water pulsed through. Pablo whipped off his baseball cap and began desperately bailing. Janella grabbed Carlos' hat from his head and did the same, but soon the water was up to Lucy's ankles.

'We'll have to swim!'

Toro's look of horror said everything she didn't want to know.

'Don't tell me . . .'

'Leave him to me,' said Rahel, already sloshing towards her little brother and his golden burden.

'Don't let go of me,' she said, hoisting Toro up. He was completely pale and his mouth trembled, but he nodded vigorously. 'And you,' he said to his monkey, 'don't let go of me!' His monkey's huge dark eyes grew even huger, as though it understood the urgency that had swamped the boat along with the water. It gave one strangled shriek and clung on even more tightly than usual.

Lucy had her own monkey to think about.

'Ricardo, if we go overboard, are you cool?'

She knew he was a good swimmer, but he was in strange waters in a strange country with soldiers shooting at them and it was her fault *again* and Mum was going to murder her this time and . . . jumping overboard seemed like a great idea.

Ricardo appeared surprisingly calm but Lucy noticed

that the hand stroking his monkey was shaking.

'Will my monkey be OK?'

'You'll just have to do your best. Monkeys can swim, can't they? Anyway, he's got a good grip on you.'

The scream of the Bulls' speedboat was suddenly horribly close. Lucy took stock. She knew Janella could swim, but what about the others?

'Pablo, can you swim?'

He paused his frantic bailing long enough to give an anguished nod.

'Carlos?'

The inquiry earned Lucy a withering look.

'Of course!'

Carlos the Zombie was back. Lucy pushed past his hostility, concern for Angel overriding her desire to tell him to jump in the river whether he could swim or not.

'Will you be OK with Angel?'

But she did not have time to hear his answer. The roar of the speedboat split the afternoon, streaking towards them. At the same time, there was a horrible groaning as another, wider crack opened in the bottom of their boat and the water washed halfway up to her knees. Rahel, with a desperate grip on Toro, stumbled to the side of the boat, their combined weight tilting it sickeningly. Staggering, she turned and shouted to the others, 'Head for the shore and then let the tide carry you to the harbour. There are lots of sailing boats there. Hide until dark, then meet me under the first jetty.'

Then she was gone. Her desperate leap was too much for Pablo. He tossed one more futile capful of water overboard, put his sodden headgear firmly back on his skull and dived after Rahel. His cap promptly fell off and floated away with the current. The last Lucy saw of Pablo was his dark head bobbing as he began an urgent breast-stroke for the shore.

'Here goes,' said Lucy. She picked up Ricardo, monkey and all, and dropped him over the side. He immediately sank and Lucy held her breath until she saw him surface, swimming strongly for the shore, which seemed a horribly long way away. A slick of golden fur clung to his back. When she looked again, Janella was gone, striking out in her strong freestyle. Lucy met Angel's eyes and froze. What was wrong with her? Any normal four-year-old would be pooping herself. Not Angel. The little girl was grinning as Carlos prepared to jump, for all the world as though she was about to embark on nothing more sinister than a ride on a giant waterslide. Carlos did not seem to share her air of celebration.

'Goodbye,' he said to Lucy and held her eyes. All trace of hostility was gone and he said his farewell as though it might have to last for a very long time.

'Goodbye,' she whispered, and suddenly wanted to cry. She was, once again, in way over her head, or she was about to be – literally. But there was no time for regret. The speedboat was so close Lucy could smell its two-stroke fuel. Then it was bearing down on their wallowing dinghy and she picked up loyal T-Tongue, threw him overboard, held her breath and dived, surrendering her fate to the River of Souls.

29

Taken

Gasping for air, Lucy burst to the surface, only to swallow a mouthful of water as an unexpected wave slapped her in the face. Where were the soldiers? When she came up again she could hear the speedboat, but it sounded further away. Another wave swamped her. When she opened her eyes, she was instantly blinded by the setting sun. That's when she realised Nature was on the children's side. Dazzled by the glare from sun and water, the soldiers were sweeping straight past, and the waves breaking over her head were from their speedboat's wake. They must have missed the broken little boat and the flotilla of children.

It wouldn't take them long to work it out, though. Treading water, Lucy cast about for the others. She could see dark heads bobbing in the water and – what was that? Yes, one dark head had already reached the shore and was dragging another smaller waterlogged body into a jungle of reeds. There was a flash of dark gold, and another tiny body disappeared after them. Rahel, Toro and an extremely damp monkey.

She felt a frantic scratch on her back and turned to meet T-Tongue's panicked gaze and scrabbling paws.

'Good boy! Come with me.'

She took another breath and struck out in the strongest freestyle jeans and joggers would allow. It didn't take her long to catch up to Ricardo and his monkey. He was paddling bravely but his white face and jagged breath told her the ordeal had exhausted him. His monkey clung to his back for dear life, waterlogged and whimpering.

'Hold on, little bro,' she panted. It was a struggle to convince the monkey to let go of Ricardo and cling to her instead, but she managed it. Then, taking Ricardo in the lifesaving grip her swimming coach had taught her, she kicked out for the shore. It seemed horribly far away.

Oh no! The whine of the speedboat was growing louder again, which meant the soldiers had doubled back. And this time, they would not be blinded by the sun. Lucy prayed that the children's boat had not yet sunk and the soldiers would waste precious time checking it out. She heard a shout and risked a backward glance. Yes! The soldiers were circling the wreckage but the wash from their speedboat was too violent. The broken craft was swallowed in a wave and sank from sight. She could see four brown-shirted forms with their backs to her, waving their arms and shouting. Then one turned and pointed upstream. Lucy followed his gaze. A small shape in the water, close to the reeds. Pablo's hat. The engine screamed into life and the soldiers sped towards the shore.

That was good for Lucy, but what about the others? Had Janella and Pablo made it? Carlos and Angel? The soldiers were way too close to where Lucy had last seen her friends' heads bobbing in the water. But there was nothing she could do. She had to get Ricardo to safety.

By the time she felt sucking mud under her shoes, she could barely breathe. Dragging Ricardo with her, she stumbled into the dubious safety of a bog with reeds stretching higher than her head in every direction – and collapsed. T-Tongue hauled himself out of the water with an exhausted whimper, licked her muddy hand and collapsed too.

And so began a terrible hour. For as long as it took for the sun to sink below the horizon, Lucy and Ricardo could hear the dread sound of the speedboat making pass after pass along the shoreline. Each time the motor whined away downstream, Lucy hoped it would be the last, but it never was. Then, just as a silky grey twilight cloaked the river, Lucy heard shouting somewhere upstream. It was too far away to hear the words, but the urgency in the voices was unmistakable. Her heart sank. It couldn't be any of the Telarian kids, they would be trying to stay silent – and there was only one thing that would get the soldiers so excited. Then a shot cracked the evening air. The speedboat roared and suddenly cut out. More shouts, another shot and then . . . a scream.

Lucy felt as though her guts had turned to muddy river water. A brutal question was a merciless jackhammer to her skull. Who? Which of her friends? *Not any of them, please . . .*

She opened her mouth to yell, but for once it was Ricardo who had more sense. He clamped his little hand over her mouth and shook his head warningly. Lucy, rigid with her terrible question, could only stare at him, eyes wide in shock and fear. Then sense slowly returned, and she nodded. He took his hand away from her mouth, and then it was his turn. His eyes filled with tears and he slumped, gently rocking the monkey whose head was buried in his chest. Then the speedboat roared back into life and Lucy grabbed his hand and pulled him lower in the reeds, squelching disgustingly down into the mud. She felt T-Tongue's cold nose against her cheek and reached out her hand to comfort him. But there was no one to comfort Lucy. No one at all.

30
Mud People

Only long, long after the dreadful growl of the speedboat had faded did Lucy gather the courage to lead her soggy little party to higher ground. Well, actually, it was T-Tongue who did the leading. With every step, Ricardo and Lucy sank to their calves into sticky, greedy mud, and it was all they could do to drag themselves forward, clinging to reeds that bent and broke. The mud squelched and sucked at their shoes and socks. T-Tongue couldn't exactly scamper ahead but his lighter frame and paws didn't sink quite as badly, either. He pushed determinedly through the reeds, and turned to face Lucy, as if to say, 'C'mon, follow me, I can get us out of here.'

Inspired, Lucy worked out that if she stamped and smashed the reeds into the mud, they formed a kind of fibrous carpet to walk on that stopped them sinking so far. But the reeds were treacherous. Their sharp blades slashed her fingers and drew blood umpteen times.

'Put your shoes and socks on your hands,' Lucy finally told Ricardo, exasperated. He wasn't so shell-shocked that he couldn't give her the 'You've got to be kidding' look, but Lucy had no patience. 'Just do it! It's the only way we're getting out of here.' She slid her own mud-encased socks and shoes onto her hands like protective gloves, and began beating a path towards T-Tongue. It worked! Ricardo stopped looking mutinous, and smashed and squelched along beside her, his monkey clinging to his back as he bent to the task.

The reeds were so tall, it was like digging a tunnel – and Lucy was grateful for that. The Bulls would not see them easily from the speedboat. But what if the Bulls had a helicopter and searchlights? The path she and Ricardo had made must look like a crazy crop circle from the air. And which of her friends had been taken?

Panic circled like a shark. Just when she thought it would swallow her whole, she felt the immeasurably welcome sensation of solid ground under her feet. She fell onto the gentle slope of the river bank and lay panting, too exhausted to move, giving mute thanks to the first stars of the Telarian evening, an impossibly bright full moon and the air heavy and sweet with the scent of ripe, golden mangoes.

Ricardo struggled onto the bank and fell down beside her. His monkey gave one enraged shriek, scrambled from his arms and leaped for the nearest tree, where it began raining down a storm of mangoes, as though furious at the ordeal it had been put through. Lucy stood to run for cover but then froze as her snake sense kicked into overdrive. The delinquent monkey must have sensed something too because it abruptly ceased its outraged screeching. In the sudden silence, Lucy closed her eyes and crouched, concentrating.

Someone was moving stealthily through the mud and reeds towards her. The mud diffused the vibration, but still it was unmistakable.

Lucy felt a wet nose on her leg and tried to give T-Tongue the silent hand-command to drop and stay – a little difficult, considering she was wearing socks and shoes on her hands. But then he was wagging his tail uncontrollably, and Lucy was seized by an irrepressible hope. Whoever was coming, T-Tongue was sure it was a friend. The reeds shuddered and shook, and by the light of the Telarian moon, Lucy saw a tiny form squelching towards her. Bravely fighting her way through the mud and reeds was . . . Angel. Alone.

31

Mango Monkey

'Angel!'

The growl of the approaching speedboat became a roar, drowning out Lucy's cry of anguish. She gathered up the little girl just as a powerful searchlight cut the night. Lucy lunged for the ground and slithered amongst the roots of an enormous mango tree, clutching Angel as though she would never let her go again. The roots of the mango stood tall, like a fence between them and the river, and Lucy hunkered down as deep as she dared, trying not to think about spiders and snakes. She felt Angel's little heart pounding against her body, as fast as a frightened bird's, and T-Tongue's wet fur against her legs.

Out beyond the barrier of mud and reeds, which suddenly seemed like old friends, the soldiers shouted excitedly. Their searchlight tracked along the trees that grew on the bank and, lying on her back, Lucy could not help watching its path. She held her breath as it passed over the tree they had taken shelter in, breathed out when it moved on, only to stop breathing altogether when, at an excited shout from the boat the beam tracked urgently back, fixing on the branches above her head.

What had they seen? A flash of gold told her what she didn't want to know. Ricardo's monkey was caught in the glare of the spotlight above her head. Her heart pumped crazily. Ricardo! – where was he? The golden monkey, outraged at the intruding spotlight, commenced a furious screeching but seemed unable to move. There was a burst of caustic laughter from the boat and Lucy's stomach tightened. She willed the monkey to move before one of the soldiers decided it would be good sport to take a shot at it.

Then, in horror, she realised she was not the only one worried. No, surely it couldn't be? Craning her neck, she saw a small white hand, reaching out from a curtain of mango leaves on the branch directly behind the monkey's perch. Stealthily, the hand grasped the monkey's tail and . . . yanked. The monkey screamed. The hand disappeared as quickly as it had appeared, but it had done its job . . . the spell was broken. Quick as a flash, the monkey twisted away from the paralysing light and grabbed the nearest mango, pelting it in the direction of the hateful laughter that still came from the boat. The next instant a snigger became a scream as one unlucky Bull took a direct hit. From her living bunker Lucy grinned, knowing exactly what was in store. But even Lucy wasn't prepared for the monkey master-stroke that followed. Smash! The searchlight shattered and darkness settled like a safety blanket.

Over the monkey's triumphant shrieking Lucy could hear the soldiers' yells of surprise and outrage.

'Good shot!' she breathed, despite herself.

The Bulls were in disarray, shouting at each other. Lucy was tempted to giggle until a harsh order silenced them. She froze. That guttural tone of command was awfully familiar. The Bull Commander! It would take more than a broken light to stop him if he'd guessed who had been in the sunken dinghy! Then it hit her. He did know – Nigel must have telephoned him after seeing her in the Telares City market!

To her intense relief, the speedboat growled grumpily and sped off. Lucy's heart did not slow its frantic beating until the sound faded away across the river. There was a rustling in the branches and Ricardo tumbled down, holding his monkey tightly. T-Tongue whimpered for joy, and once again Lucy was moved to pay her little brother a compliment.

'I never thought I'd say this, bro, but that monkey rocks!'

'I reckon,' said Ricardo shakily, and promptly burst into tears. 'They were going to shoot him!'

His distress did what it always did for Lucy: it brought out her protective streak and made her realise that once again she was in charge, whether she liked it or not. It was up to her to get them all out of this mess. In the moonlight, she looked from her little brother to Angel and back again. The little girl had not made a sound since the speedboat arrived and was still clinging to Lucy. Lucy was reminded of how withdrawn Angel had been when she was first rescued from the jungle jail, after spending months chained up to that horrible loom. Since her release, Angel had blossomed. Now Lucy sensed it had all been undone. Angel had shrunk back into herself, looking even smaller than usual. The thought sent Lucy into a shaking, silent rage.

Damn the Bull Commander! Just when they were so close to getting Angel home to her grandparents, he had got in the way again. And now Nigel had the rug that Angel had wanted to take home so badly. Then Lucy remembered Carlos, and her blood turned to ice.

'Angel, where is Carlos?'

But the little girl just turned away. Lucy's head began to pound horribly, but from a great distance, as though her neck had been stretched and her head was stranded somewhere up near the top of the trees, where a giant bashed her about the ears with a monstrous hammer. Lucy fought and conquered the scream of panic that rose in her throat. Taking deep breaths, gradually she regained control and, when her head had stopped ringing and appeared to be firmly back on her shoulders, she welcomed a familiar fizz of fury in her feet. Her head suddenly clear, she faced the two smaller children with a determined expression. Yes, this was a time to be angry. But on her terms.

'OK,' she said calmly, 'this is what we have to do.'

32

The Journey

Lucy led her bedraggled party of two small children, a dog and a monkey through the trees until the moonlight revealed a faint sandy path winding above the bank.

'Come on, the harbour can't be that far,' she lied bravely. She settled Angel on her shoulders and started off, T-Tongue heeling obediently and Ricardo trotting to keep up, his monkey tucked sleepily into his shoulder.

In the end it wasn't so hard. The moon reflected gently off the soft sand of the path and it was easy to keep to the track. Lucy felt her cat senses stir and stretch, and once again the night became her friend, a place to prowl, silent and proud.

Once along the way, another sense kicked in and she stopped suddenly, dragging Ricardo and Angel into deeper cover and putting her palms on the ground. Her head pounded in time with the undeniable vibration of approaching feet, but T-Tongue began to wag his tail and gave an excited whimper of recognition. The first to join them was Pablo, clothes and hair plastered flat with mud.

Then Lucy's snake sense detected more feet, and soon T-Tongue welcomed Rahel, clutching Janella's hand. Then Ricardo's monkey gave a strangled shriek and Toro and his golden friend emerged from behind a tree.

It should have been a joyful reunion, but it wasn't.

'Carlos?' was all Lucy could manage. Rahel swallowed a sob and turned away, dashing Lucy's last stubborn hope. The low growl of the speedboat was almost a relief, washing dumb misery away in a burst of adrenalin. Children and animals melted into the scrub. The engine cut out and a searchlight probed the trees lining the bank, but it was too far upstream to be any real threat.

Rahel jerked her head at Lucy. 'Let's get out of here,' she meant, and Lucy was in no mood to argue. The party padded away from the searchlight, not daring to walk on the path, but sheltering in the trees instead. Their progress was painfully slow, punctuated with terrifying moments as the speedboat roared closer, only to stop so the light could rake the river trees. But the children managed to stay a jump ahead. It seemed to take forever until Lucy finally rounded a bend to find, spread out below, the lights of a harbour. It still looked horribly far away.

Now Rahel quickened her pace and took the lead. The trees had begun to thin, so she snuck from trunk to trunk, motioning for the others to come forward when she was sure the coast was clear. Soon the smell of salt water was unmistakable. After a while the path sloped down towards the sandy beach lining the harbour itself, leaving the sheltering trees behind. No one liked that at all and, as one, the group stopped dead in the last meagre shadows.

They could still hear the speedboat, the soldiers gunning the motor every few minutes to search a fresh stretch of bank, drawing inexorably closer to the harbour.

Rahel's voice shook but Lucy could sense her determination. 'We have no choice,' she said. 'If we go now, there are many places to hide on the harbour – an empty vessel, a boatshed. If we stay here, by the morning they will have a platoon of Bulls combing this forest and eventually they will find us. Our best chance is to get to Angel's grandparents' home.'

'But it will take us many hours,' countered Pablo.

'So be it,' was Rahel's steely rejoinder.

'Let's go,' said Lucy grimly and fell in behind her, with Angel on her back and Janella by her side. The Kurrawong girl looked shaken, wet and bedraggled, but she tried to give Lucy a brave grin, and Lucy was grateful for it. They crept down the path, feeling horribly exposed, but no shouts or shots greeted them. The Bulls were still busy upstream. It seemed to be an eternity before Rahel led them under the welcome shadow of the first jetty. Peering out from a barnacle-encrusted pier, Lucy saw jetty after jetty, each with boats small and large, ramshackle and luxurious, bobbing at anchor. The children snuck through shallow water, keeping to the shadows of the jetties, putting as much distance between themselves and that relentless searchlight as they could.

Lucy knew it would not be long before the Bulls began searching the harbour itself. The children needed to get away – fast. Just as the thought formed, an odd-shaped boat tied to the end of the jetty next to the one they were skulking beneath caught her eye. Most of the boats were dark or just had one light burning, but this one was lit up like a Christmas tree.

On closer inspection, it didn't look like a boat at all. It was quite large and square, like a shoebox. A houseboat, it was a houseboat! How cool! What was not cool was the sudden roar of the speedboat, much closer than before. The searchlight knifed along the first jetty, lingering on every pier, lighting up the dark spaces where the children had been hiding only moments earlier. Lucy's legs turned rubbery and she felt she could no longer walk.

Suddenly, every light on the houseboat was extinguished, but not before Lucy saw a small shape leap gracefully across the gangway and up the jetty. A familiar purr warmed the night. Lucy did not need T-Tongue's whimper of nervous delight to tell her who was waiting across that small stretch of shallow water. The Tiger-cat gave an urgent growl as if to say 'Hurry!' With a terrified look over her shoulder, Lucy slipped through the shadows to the other jetty and clambered up, holding Angel awkwardly, horribly conscious of how visible she would be if that searchlight swung in her direction. Then a warm, furry body was rubbing about her legs and she felt an eruption of hope for the first time in an ice age of fear. Next, another shock! A low and strangely familiar voice whispered from the darkness near the houseboat, 'You children would be advised to climb aboard. Hurry now! We don't have much time.'

Lucy froze, but the voice seemed to be a signal for the Tiger-cat to streak back towards the boat. And Angel – Angel struggled violently and had wriggled down onto the jetty before Lucy knew what was happening. Then she was gone, her little feet pattering after the Tiger-cat and towards that mysterious voice.

'Angel!' Lucy hissed desperately, but it was the haunting voice which answered, even more urgently, 'You must trust me.'

The searchlight arced once more into the sky and settled down to search the second pier. Lucy could hear the Bulls barking orders. Trust who? Where had she heard that voice before? But what choice did they have? They couldn't leave Angel behind.

Rahel clambered up next to her to confer in a breathless hurry.

'You must come!' said the voice and Rahel took one more look at the speedboat and leaned over the jetty and urged the others to climb up. Then she was tiptoeing towards the houseboat. Lucy grabbed T-Tongue's collar and Ricardo's hand and followed. They reached the gangway just as the speedboat charged towards the third jetty. Luckily, the children were hidden by the hulking shape of the houseboat. Rahel was already skidding across the gangway. Throwing caution to the winds, Lucy put one foot on its swaying planks and then she was stepping into the dark entrance of what could very well be a trap. Only the Tiger-cat's welcoming purr reassured her. Pablo, bringing up the rear, had the presence of mind to lift the gangway after them and then the door shut tight and that strangely familiar voice whispered, from a blanketing darkness that smelled unexpectedly of kerosene and toast, 'Welcome.'

A torch flashed, briefly illuminating stairs plunging below deck. 'I think it would be better if you were discreet,' the voice said. Lucy grabbed Angel by the hand.

The little girl struggled and tried to say something but Lucy propelled her towards the stairs as the speedboat roared closer. And then, horror, the searchlight raked across the houseboat itself, slashing crazy lines through the cracks in the curtains. The children didn't need a second warning and soon the group was huddled downstairs, barely breathing, as heavy boots pounded along the jetty and a harsh voice shouted at the door.

To Lucy's absolute terror, the door of the houseboat swung open. She had the distinct impression that their tense silence below decks could itself be heard. There was a brusque query from a soldier and then the low voice of the mysterious pilot of the houseboat. Whoever it was did not sound worried at all. Lucy felt a scrabbling next to her and a furry body pushed past her and up the stairs to the upper deck. A miaow floated below decks and then, shock horror, the Bull soldier and the houseboat owner were laughing. After a cheerful farewell, the door closed firmly, and she could hear the soldier's heavy boots thump back along the jetty. The speedboat roared away. Why was the Bull so happy? Were they caught in a trap?

The stairs shook and the Tiger-cat's purring filled the cabin. A light flooded on, dazzling the children. 'Tea and toast?' asked a cheerful voice. Blinking, Lucy looked at their saviour. 'Nina?' she whispered incredulously. The crinkly woman with the ginger eyes and the white plait coiled high smiled gently and opened her mouth to speak. But Angel got there first. She struggled from Lucy's arms, charged across the cabin and flung herself at the old woman with an exultant cry. 'Grandmama!'

33
Houseboating

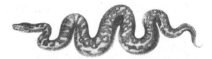

Over Angel's head the old woman's crinkly eyes smiled into Lucy's. Lucy searched her face. No, not Nina, but surely . . . ?

The old woman seemed to follow her thoughts and chuckled. 'Yes, Lucia, you are right. There is a resemblance, yes?'

She spoke with old-fashioned courtesy, head tilted graciously, and stood, even leaning on a walking stick, with the bearing of an elderly queen. Lucy was so overwhelmed by the likeness she did not notice the use of her name, let alone the pet name that only Dad and Nina called her.

Not so Ricardo. 'How do you know her name?' he shot suspiciously at the dignified old woman.

'And you must be Ricardo,' was her reply, sending him into a wide-eyed silence. Lucy liked her already.

'But this is no time for questions,' the old woman said. 'You must eat. You have come a long, long way, after all. And' – the old woman paused – 'from the bottom of my heart, I thank you for bringing my granddaughter back to me.' She walked stiffly to an armchair in the corner of the cabin and settled the little girl on her lap, examining her as a jeweller would a precious stone that had been stolen and returned.

'I knew you would come back,' she whispered and kissed her on both cheeks. At that, Angel turned her head and met Lucy's eyes. 'Lucy did take Angel home. Lucy did!'

Her comment punctured the tension and a relieved giggle fluttered through the cabin. Lucy saw Rahel's brief smile and realised she had not seen it for a very long time. Then, just as quickly, a curtain of grief fell over her friend's face, and Lucy too was plunged back into despair at Carlos' fate.

The old woman noticed her expression. 'But you are in trouble, yes? Never fear. I may be able to help. But now,' she said firmly, 'food before talk.' She perched Angel on the arm of the chair and disappeared through a tiny door. Soon the smell of toast filled the cabin.

'Janella and Pablo? I wonder if I could have your assistance in here?'

The two teenagers hesitated, and then walked obediently into the galley, emerging a few seconds later with inviting trays. Lucy, sick with fear for Carlos, did not think she could eat, but the sight of hot buttered toast after her ordeal on the river changed her mind. She realised she had not eaten since they left Kurrawong – and that felt like a year ago. As they sipped hot, sweet, milky tea, the old woman spoke.

'If you are surprised that I know your situation, don't be.

I know that Lucy noticed an undeniable likeness to my twin sister Nina. Between Nina and Euphoria, here,' she stroked the Tiger-cat's marmalade fur affectionately, 'I remain abreast of events – on many planes.' She shot a bright, knowing look at the children, one by one.

'It was I who arranged for the little boat to be moored on the River of Souls at your convenience. My name is Madam Eleanor and thanks to Euphoria I feel I know all of you already.' Her face clouded. 'I notice one particular angry young man is missing. What happened to Carlos?'

Lucy broke the bruising silence. 'The Bulls took him.' Even as she spoke she realised she was desperate to know exactly what had happened to him. Earlier it had been enough to know that he was gone – what else mattered? Now, for some reason, she needed every awful detail.

'What happened?' she pleaded, locking eyes with Rahel.

The Telarian girl answered heavily. 'He did not make it ashore. He was swimming with Angel when the speedboat came. We had reached the rushes and were hiding. They did not see us. He managed to get Angel close to the rushes and pushed her into the mud. He told her to hide. But the soldiers saw him and began shooting. They swept up and plucked him from the water like a fish. He screamed and struggled. And . . .', her voice shook, 'he was covered in blood.'

Once again Lucy had that sensation of her head being separated from her body. She heard herself from a long way away asking incredulously, 'They shot him?'

Rahel nodded dumbly and Pablo made an inarticulate

choking sound and turned to face the wall. At the sight of Lucy's stricken face, Rahel seemed to dredge up some courage. Her voice firmed and she put her hand on the Kurrawong girl's arm.

'He is not dead! I know it. He had the strength to struggle. We could hear him shouting at them halfway across the river. He was very rude!'

Lucy agreed that was indeed a good sign, and Rahel continued.

'He struggled so much that he almost upset the boat. As for Angel, they knew she was there but she wriggled deep into the rushes. We had to stay very still or they would have seen us too. And when night fell we searched and searched, but we could not find her, and the boat kept returning. We had to leave.'

'Angel found Lucy,' the little girl piped up.

But Lucy was remembering something. 'The Bull Commander. I heard his voice when we were hiding in the trees. Did he shoot Carlos?'

'No, they were just soldiers. But then they sped back to Telares City and returned with a searchlight. The Bull Commander must have come with them. And he will interrogate Carlos.' On these last words, Rahel's voice broke.

'He will not speak,' said Pablo harshly.

Rahel shook her head sadly. 'He will not want to speak, but the Bulls, they have their ways. You know what the Bull Commander is capable of, Pablo.' Pablo seemed to shrink inside his skin.

Lucy could not stand it.

'Listen. I don't care what happens, we're getting him

out. Even if they don't hurt him any more, it will kill him to be a prisoner again. And he is terrified of the Bull Commander. You remember what happened in the cubby.' Lucy's voice was shrill. She took a deep breath and calmed herself, feeling once again that tingling in her toes. When she spoke again, her voice was resolute and confident. 'He will need medical treatment. And besides, I've got a plan.'

But Madam Eleanor interrupted. 'You can tell us about it later, my dear. Right now, it is not safe to stay on the river. You must come back to Pasadena Square. This brave young man came to my granddaughter's assistance and gave up his freedom for hers. I will do everything in my power to help you.'

As the speedboat grumbled in the distance, Lucy looked at the old woman with her walking stick and lined face and could not help a silent disrespect. *Well, you're a nice old duck, but you and whose army?*

Lucy peered out a window. The searchlight continued to probe the jetties downstream.

'Will the Bulls come back?' she asked Madam Eleanor.

'Perhaps, and that is why it is important to cast off. I put them off before without much trouble, but if they get bored and frustrated when they do not find you, they may not be so well-mannered.'

'How did you get rid of them?'

'They had seen some movement on the jetty but I told them it was just my houseboy bringing the cat inside, and Euphoria chose that moment to come upstairs and illus-trate my point.' Her eyes twinkled and she looked very much like Nina. 'I can be a very polite old sailor when I choose. So, he apologised, thanked me for my time and left a tired old lady alone, but not before he told me who they were looking for: a group of young criminals, some of them illegal immigrants.' This last was delivered with a meaningful glance at Lucy, Ricardo and Janella. 'But I must ask you – there were a few items Euphoria suggested you might have for me?'

Lucy scrabbled in her backpack, grateful something had gone right.

'Nina asked me to give these to you,' she said, handing over the tiger pattern in its envelope and the leather pouch that held the dragon chest key. Madam Eleanor's face lit up and she quickly put them in her voluminous handbag.

Lucy knew she had to confess. 'But there's more bad news. Angel wanted us to bring the rug and we got it all the way to Telares City and then Nigel Scar-Skull saw us and the soldiers chased us and now Nigel's got the rug.'

Madam Eleanor grew very still. 'Nigel,' she said thoughtfully. 'That is indeed a setback.' Then she shook herself and continued briskly, 'But we must hurry. If you will excuse me.' She hobbled upstairs and soon the houseboat engine grumbled into life, throbbing beneath their feet like a giant heart. For Lucy and Rahel, snake senses fully awake, the unfamiliar vibration was so intense it was almost painful. They exchanged an understanding glance and climbed up on the seats under the windows to watch through the cracks in the curtains as the lights of Telares City drew closer. It was beautiful: a blinking, winking, welcoming fairyland. Looking at her friend, Lucy surprised tears in Rahel's eyes, quickly dashed away.

'It has been a long time,' was all she said.

34

Pasadena Square

The houseboat puttered past a fleet of expensive yachts anchored in the middle of the harbour. It was heading towards the far side of the river, which was lined with gracious old mansions, many lit up like castles. Their gardens swept down to the water, and each had a private jetty and boats. But the house Madam Eleanor steered them to was in darkness – a great hulking shadow, several storeys high, set back from the river.

The vessel bumped gently against the jetty and then the old woman stiffly but expertly threw a rope over the mooring post. She turned to the children gathered at the top of the stairs and her kindly face had grown suddenly hard.

'You must not be seen. The city is riddled with spies. The neighbours . . . well, they are not exactly neighbourly. Bull officers and their families have taken over many of these old homes. Now, to the door, very quietly.'

Lucy peered out at a brightly lit stately old mansion on her left, separated from Madam Eleanor's home by a high hedge. Through open French windows she could see someone walking around upstairs. She caught her breath. The man was in uniform. A brown uniform. The evening was warm and Lucy could see people having drinks on a balcony, even hear the clink of glasses and the tinkle of laughter. Cheerful lot, the Bulls, when they weren't arresting kids.

The old woman saw her anxiety. 'Yes, so you see . . . I'm afraid I'm going to have to ask you to get wet again. Slip over the side one by one and swim to the end of the jetty. Once you reach the cover of the hedge, you should be able to sneak up our path without being noticed. The back door is open and my husband Eduardo will be waiting for you. He is very statuesque but please don't be afraid. Euphoria is very fond of him. And, if you don't mind, dear, when you get inside, would you mind running a bath.'

This humorous suggestion to a mud-splattered Pablo broke the ice. With a brave grin, he dropped silently into the water. One by one the others followed. Angel clung to her grandmama for a long moment, but the old woman gently disentangled her.

'I am sorry, my darling. If the neighbours see you, we are lost. You must swim to Grandpapa with Lucy.'

'It's cool, Angel,' whispered Lucy and the little girl slipped obediently into the water with her. Once again Lucy struck out for a strange shore. They reached the safety of the hedge, shivering, and watched the old woman and the Tiger-cat walk openly along the jetty and wish a cheery greeting to someone in the neighbouring garden.

Then the hugest man Lucy had ever seen stepped from

the shadows near the door and picked up Angel. He clapped a hand over her mouth to prevent her crying out and ushered Lucy and the others inside wordlessly. He was a towering tree of a Telarian, with massive shoulders. He was also totally bald, and somehow had found a black ninja suit to fit him, and black slippers. Yet, despite his height and weight, he moved with absolute silence. He lifted Angel to the light as though to see her better, and the sleeve of his suit slipped back, revealing a tattoo of a tiger on his impressive forearm.

'Grandpapa!' Angel cried and, watching his face closely, Lucy saw that even giants cried. He wiped the tears away and turned to his unexpected guests.

'Eduardo,' said Madam Eleanor, 'I would like to introduce you to Nina's gifts to us. Bright young company for a lonely old house.'

She introduced the children one by one. Nothing could have prepared them for the experience of shaking Angel's granddad's hand. Their tiny palms were swallowed in his mighty yet surprisingly gentle grip. But he was a man of few words and long silences.

'Thank you for returning my beloved granddaughter,' was all he said before he vanished on silent feet into the shadows of the hallway.

Madam Eleanor turned reassuringly to the children. 'Now, my dears, you have come a long way and are wet, cold and hungry. We will organise baths, fresh clothes. And, after you are refreshed, you have my word, we will find out what has happened to your friend.'

'How?' snapped Rahel, uncharacteristically brusque, but Madam Eleanor just smiled calmly.

Lucy too was brimming with questions. 'And what about Nina, do you know where she is? Nigel Scar-Skull is going to bulldoze the Mermaid House. He says she is dead. He even put it in the paper!'

Now that got Madam Eleanor's attention. 'Dead? How very dramatic of our lovely nephew.' She refused to say more. 'Please, I insist you eat.'

She would not be swayed, and if the truth be told it did not take much to convince the children, once they had washed, to eat Eduardo's coconut curry and rice. He had even found them ninja suits in various sizes that almost gave Ricardo and Toro palpitations.

Only when the last spoonful had disappeared did Madam Eleanor relent.

'Now, I will show you how we can track down your friend.'

She led the way through a series of rooms lined with antique lamps and dusty paintings.

'You must forgive the state of this place. It used to be full of people and children but these days it is just myself and Eduardo and' – she leaned down to stroke the Tiger-cat's fur – 'Euphoria on her occasional visits.'

Halfway down a dark passage, Eduardo bent, rolling a rug aside to reveal a trapdoor. It opened smoothly, as though it had been regularly used, and he flicked on a light to reveal stairs plunging below. Down, down, down they climbed, until Lucy was sure they must have gone beneath the very harbour. It was like being back in the tunnel. The air grew musty and Lucy half-imagined they were heading for Madam Eleanor's own version of the cubby. She was totally unprepared for the sight that

184

greeted her when Eduardo opened a padlocked door at the bottom of the stairs and turned on the light. The hum her cat-ears had noticed, rising in intensity as they approached, suddenly made sense. A bank of computers took up an entire wall of what should have been a dungeon but was in fact an exceedingly modern room, with modems blinking, printers humming, faxes rolling.

The children could only stare, open-mouthed. Clearly enjoying their amazement, Madam Eleanor marched to a very swish flat-screen set-up that Lucy would have died to have at home, and began tapping furiously.

Her modem began blinking just as furiously and after a minute the old lady gave a gentle sigh of satisfaction. 'Ah,' she said, happily, 'I will give our Bulls this much: they are efficient and they keep excellent records. It will not be long before I have the information you need.'

Obviously enjoying their flabbergasted expressions, Madam Eleanor finally took pity on the children. 'It is very simple. Euphoria has her talents and I have mine. Euphoria told me you were in trouble tonight and where to find you. And now it is my turn to tell you where your friend is – using the rather more prosaic talents of one humble hacker.' She bowed her head, as though offering her services, but could not quite hide a mischievous smile.

'A hacker!' they chorused.

The old woman nodded breezily.

'It's not just for the young, you know. What better activity for an old lady who can't run marathons any more? I must have a hobby. But, down to business.' She turned back to the computer and for a few moments the only sound was the tapping of her flying fingers. Then she gave a satisfied sigh.

'Yes, you have created quite a stir. The Bulls are going to great trouble with this particular prisoner. They have taken him to hospital.'

'Hospital?' That didn't make sense to Lucy. Had the Bulls suddenly developed a caring streak? Then she saw the set looks on her Telarian friends' faces and understood the ugly truth.

'The Commander wants him alive, doesn't he?' she whispered.

'Yes, my dear,' agreed Madam Eleanor regretfully, 'tomorrow, at dawn, Carlos Xavier Romero is scheduled for transfer to . . .'

Rahel could no longer contain herself. She pushed past Lucy to the screen. She read the words under her breath and gave a cry of distress that sent a chill down Lucy's spine. Rahel spoke rapidly to Pablo in Telarian. He sat down heavily on the ground, clenching and unclenching his fists. Toro squeezed his monkey so hard it squeaked.

Only the old woman seemed unmoved. 'Now, now, it is too soon to panic.'

Rahel turned to her, and spoke furiously in Telarian.

'Yes, my dear, but it is a long time until morning,' the old woman said placidly.

'What?' cried Lucy, hugely frustrated, a knot of fear winding tighter and tighter in her belly. 'Tell me what's going on!'

Rahel spat the words out. 'He is under guard in the hospital tonight, which is bad enough, but tomorrow he will be taken to the Telares City Tower for interrogation.

And the order has been signed by the Bull Commander himself. He is considered a person of "special interest".'

'What is the Tower?'

A deep voice rumbled ominously, 'The young madam does not want to know.' Eduardo, stood, arms akimbo, at the door, as if ready to fell anyone who entered uninvited. If Lucy had not seen his lips move, she would have thought he was carved from stone.

'I'm afraid my husband is not overstating the case,' Madam Eleanor said quietly. 'It would go very much better for your friend if he was, shall we say, liberated, before he reached the Tower. Those who go in tend not to come out.'

Lucy's fingers and toes fizzed with enough electric anger to light up a small town. But her head was very clear. And in that moment she learned something: when all your choices telescope down to just one life-and-death chance, it makes your decisions easy. Dead easy.

'What time are they moving him?' she asked Rahel.

'Dawn,' was the steely answer.

'Righto,' said Lucy. The girls locked eyes.

35

The Secret
of the Rug

Everyone trooped back upstairs to sit in comfortable if
dusty armchairs to plan Carlos' rescue. Madam Eleanor
and Eduardo were not like most adults. They listened
quietly as each child had their say – and they did not try to
talk them out of their mission.

'I would like to prevent you from taking any risks, but
everything has been turned upside down here in Telares,'
Madam Eleanor sighed. 'The Bulls do not respect children.
They put them to work in their terrible factories. They
separate them from their loved ones,' with a glance at
Angel, 'and they destroy their communities. The people
who should help children, the authorities, now harm
them. In these circumstances, children only have each
other. Carlos will die if you do not intercept his transfer to
the Tower. We have only one stipulation: Angel does not
take part.'

There was a collective intake of breath.

'Of course not,' said Lucy, outraged. 'Our job was to get
her back safely to you.'

'For which I thank you. Now, Eduardo and I will do whatever we can to help. And,' with a glance at Rahel and Pablo, 'it is not too late to enlist some rebel support.'

'No,' said Rahel sharply. 'We have caused them enough trouble by running away. We act alone.'

Madam Eleanor and Eduardo exchanged a meaningful look but kept listening.

Only at midnight, their planning done and the little ones beginning to yawn, did Lucy feel brave enough to ask the questions she had been longing to. They spilled out in a torrent.

'Please, Madam Eleanor, what is happening to us? Ever since I moved into the Mermaid House, things have gone crazy. I keep having these psycho dreams. We found the Tiger-cat. There's a carpet growing itself alive in my bedroom, just like the one Angel was making. We got lost in a tunnel to another country. I'm turning into a tiger – when I'm not a bat or a snake! Janella's started to talk to a horse. And why is Nigel Scar-Skull such a creep? Sorry – I shouldn't have said that, he's your relative. But why does he want the pattern for the rug so much? He got really mad when we wouldn't give him the dragon chest. As for Angel, I know she's your granddaughter and I love her, but actually she's a complete weirdo!'

Lucy had a million more questions but had run out of words and, if the truth be told, had confused herself just a little. But Madam Eleanor looked not in the least concerned.

'I agree,' said Madam Eleanor with a gentle smile. 'It is time for a bedtime story that will answer some of your questions.'

Eduardo made cups of hot chocolate and gave up his

position guarding the door to sit in the largest armchair of all, ready for the story. Lucy held her breath and caught Janella's eye. Maybe they would finally get some answers? Ricardo and Toro sat up straight, determined to stay awake, but their monkeys were drooped drowsily over their shoulders. The Tiger-cat, of course, picked that moment to stroll through the door and leap onto Angel's lap. To the accompaniment of rich purring, Madam Eleanor began.

'Once upon a time, before Telares was even Telares, there was a carpet. A new king ordered it be woven to celebrate his coronation. Every species – every bird, every animal, every flower – was to be represented in one glorious rug. It was to be made of the finest silk and he summoned the most skilful weaver in the land.

'That weaver was a young woman of exceptional talent and exquisite sensitivity. She was honoured to serve her new king, even if it meant leaving her two small children for many hours each day to toil on the loom. And she had another more pressing reason: the weaver loved the creatures and the wild places of her island – but feared this king did not. Since he had ascended the throne, his men had been destroying the forests and selling the trees and the plants and animals who sheltered amongst them. The people of the island had always taken a little here and there, but only what they needed and never enough to cause real harm. But now the king's men were taking so much, the forests were shrinking and the creatures had nowhere to live. The weaver hoped to soften the king's heart by showing him how beautiful his island was.

'She wove from the soul, and her concentration was such that when she wove a bird, she imagined she was caressing real feathers. When she wove a tiger, it was as if she were stroking real fur. But of course, this was just an artist's illusion. The carpet was just a carpet. Even so, the soldiers guarding her work knew they were watching the birth of a masterpiece.

'But the king was a wicked king. As it neared completion, he too understood the weaver had created an astounding treasure. What if another king saw its glory and wanted one too? His heart was filled with greed and he vowed this sight would be seen by one king alone.

'On the day the carpet was completed he summoned the weaver. He congratulated her on her magnificent work and said she could give it any name she chose. The shy weaver bowed her head and whispered, "Your Highness, I wish to call it the Carpet of All Creation. I have tried to weave the joy of all creatures, all things, into this humble carpet."

'"So be it," he ordered, and she was filled with gratitude.

'But then,' Madam Eleanor's tone was ominous, 'came the wicked king's terrible commandment. He ordered that the pattern of the carpet be destroyed – and that the woman who had created it be executed. He commanded his servants to lock the carpet in a vault, with armed guards outside so no one but he could cast eyes upon it.

'The weaver begged and pleaded, and promised that she would never reveal the pattern to anyone – but the king was implacable. Finally, accepting that she could not sway him and she would die in the morning, the weaver made one final request: let her spend her last night with her children and husband. But again he refused, lest she reveal the pattern to them.

'"Then," said the weaver, suddenly very calm, "allow me to spend my last night locked up, alone with the rug I have given my life for."

'The king could see no reason not to grant her request – but that moment of mercy was his undoing.

'The weaver shed many tears that night. She had a loving heart that was born to bring joy and life into the world – and she cried for all the carpets she would never make. She cried for all the plants and birds and animals she would not see again. She cried for the forest she would never walk in. She cried for the husband who was so proud of her. She cried for her son and daughter, who would miss her so much. She cried for the sun and the moon and the stars. She cried for night and for day. She cried tears of anger and sadness. And finally, she cried tears of joy, because she had lived life with her eyes open. She had seen all the beauty around her and tried to show it to others in her carpets. And she knew her carpet was a work of love.

'A million tears fell into the carpet's silken pile, and when the guards came to escort her to her death at sunrise, a brave guard risked one last forbidden look – and saw something extraordinary had happened.' Madam Eleanor's voice was hushed and the children leaned forward, not taking their eyes from her face. 'All the animals and plants, the pattern woven so carefully into weft and warp, had disappeared. The weaver's tears had washed all the colour from the silk thread. The priceless Carpet of All Creation was just an old, plain rug, the kind you could trade at the bazaar for a sack of rice and throw down on a dirt floor.

'Trembling, the guard informed the king, who strode into the locked room to find the weaver sitting cross-legged, red-eyed but smiling peacefully, on nothing but a shabby old brown carpet.

'Of course, the king murdered the weaver immediately and he was so furious at the destruction of his rug that he ordered it be thrown away. So the guards wrapped the weaver's body in the rug and returned it to her family.

'The guards told them she was killed because she had woven an ugly carpet. Her family unwrapped her body and saw it was true. But that same brave guard remained behind to tell them the truth, and they shed tears of grief and love on the ruined masterpiece.

'That night, the rain began to fall. At first, it was as gentle as the tears of a girl and no one took much notice. But it rained all night and by sunrise, exactly twenty-four hours after the weaver's execution, the rain was a torrent – as intense as the tears of a doomed woman.

'It poured until the mighty River of Souls burst its banks and the king's palace was flooded. Word soon spread that the murderous king was being punished for his evil act, and worse, that he had doomed his people with him. Afraid of the rain and his people's wrath, the king ordered his guards to row him across the swollen river to higher ground. It would do him no good for, halfway across, the king saw a figure walking towards him, through the fog, over the water. As the figure drew closer, he saw it was a woman, crying an ocean of tears. His guilty heart told him who it was. He dived into the flooded river to escape and not one of his guards chose to help. When he drowned that day in the River of Souls, the rain stopped.

'It was then that the weaver's two small children, sobbing on the old brown rug for their mother, noticed something strange: as the sun came from behind the clouds, their beloved mother's carpet began to glow. Soon, the Carpet of All Creation was back, in all its silken glory. Then, the legend goes, their mother appeared to them and said her farewells.

'And,' Madam Eleanor again lowered her voice, 'she gave them certain instructions.

'The children tried to show their father and grand-parents how beautiful the Carpet of All Creation really was – but, blind with grief, the adults could not see the pattern. The children were the only ones who could. Then, remembering their mother's instructions, they begged to be allowed to keep the old brown rug.

'And that glorious pattern has been in my family ever since. See.' Madam Eleanor indicated the rug beneath their feet.

Lucy gazed uncomprehendingly at the shabby old specimen. It was just an ordinary old rug, in faded browns. But then it was as though she were looking at one of those optical illusions at Dad's Science Centre – she squinted and the faint markings on the shabby rug resolved into . . . 'A tiger rug!' she exclaimed.

'A Carpet of All Creation,' Madam Eleanor corrected her gently, 'a very old faded one. My family has been weaving them since my ancestor was put to death. Those two motherless children grew up to be master weavers –.and, following their mother's wishes, they vowed that the

Carpet of All Creation should be shared with the world, not kept locked up for one greedy person. They created a detailed pattern, to be passed down to each generation in the family – with the proviso that carpets made from it could never be sold, but must be given away to public galleries and museums for all the people of the world to see. The family could sell any rug except a Carpet of All Creation.

'This went on for many generations. And many carpets were made and given to the people. But every several hundred years, a weaver in the family would create a Carpet of All Creation that not everyone could see. Some children and a very rare adult would be able to see the pattern, but to everyone else it would appear old and shabby. These carpets were known as Invisible Creations. And it was noticed that the children and few adults who could see the carpets all developed special talents and a unique ability to commune with the creatures woven into them.

'The children of the original weaver had done their job well. They had left behind manuscripts telling the old stories. And so it was, that those in my family with eyes to see the Invisible Creations always understood them as a warning from our ancestor that a wicked leader was steering the island to disaster. Those who could see them had a task – to create another Carpet of All Creation as quickly as possible to save the island.

'Lucy, I understand you have seen Nina's atlas?'

Lucy nodded. That wacky atlas had bugged her since summer. It was filled with islands shaped exactly like Telares, each with a different name. They were scattered around the world, and each had a different date written next to it, hundreds of years apart. But when Lucy looked at an ordinary atlas, the only island of that distinctive shape was Telares, right on the International Date Line.

'Nina is worried,' Madam Eleanor continued. 'For years she studied our family's ancient manuscripts and the historical documents at the Telares Museum. That is where she met her husband Theodore. He was a visiting Australian archaeologist who specialised in natural disasters. He studied Telarian legends about great waves and floods and then looked for evidence to see if they were true. He found proof of several disasters – and then he cross-checked with Nina's documents.

'All the disasters,' Madam Eleanor's voice was hushed again, 'had one thing in common – they always occurred under a greedy, cruel leader who plundered the island, just as the Bulls are doing now. Theodore argued that this was mere coincidence – but Nina believed otherwise. She went back to the family manuscripts and realised the disasters not only occurred after an Invisible Creation appeared, but also after a greedy leader had stolen a Carpet of All Creation in order to grow rich! And, before each disaster, the family had tried to complete a new Carpet of All Creation – but had failed.

'And that's when Nina found her atlas buried in the dustiest corner of the museum – but when she showed it to Theodore, he couldn't see it! He thought the pages were blank! Nina was immediately reminded of the Invisible Creations and decided the atlas, too, was a warning.

'She gave Theodore the latitude and longitude of all the islands shaped like Telares in the atlas, and the dates recorded next to them. And her hunch was correct! Theodore found that a terrible disaster had befallen each island on those dates – they had been drowned in a torrent of rain, or broken by an earthquake, or swamped in a tsunami, or a volcano had erupted. The islands and their people had disappeared without a trace.'

Lucy could not help interrupting, 'But why were they all shaped just like Telares?'

'We fear the atlas is warning us the same fate awaits Telares soon – unless we take action,' said Madam Eleanor.

'If there's an earthquake or a landslide under the sea, there is nothing we can do to prevent a tsunami,' Rahel said gloomily.

'Correct, but we can prepare. The Bulls would save themselves and they would do nothing for the Telarians.'

Rahel nodded, but she still appeared dubious.

'There is more, my dear,' said Madam Eleanor kindly. 'In 1600, the date recorded next to Telares itself on the last printed page of the atlas, there was a tsunami here, not strong enough to destroy the island, but strong enough to inundate the coastal areas. Nina checked again, and sure enough, the king and queen at the time had taken to trading tiger skins and golden monkey brains.' Madam Eleanor paused until Ricardo stopped pretending to vomit. 'And when Nina consulted the family records she saw that not only had an Invisible Creation been made shortly before the disaster, but the greedy rulers had sent soldiers to steal a Carpet of All Creation and had sold it for a huge sum to the English royal family.

'However – and this is the lesson – the weaver who had made the Invisible Creation was a scholar of the old teachings. After the theft, he immediately began work on a new Carpet of All Creation.

'He had also developed an intense relationship with the creatures depicted in his carpets, particularly elephants. When he walked down the street, working elephants would trumpet a greeting. And, the day before the tsunami struck – he knew it was going to happen!'

'How!'

'The family elephant told him,' Madam Eleanor said, as though it were the most obvious conclusion. The kids' blank faces appeared to amuse her.

'The elephant suggested quite strongly to him that it was time to head for the hills. That she would appreciate it a great deal if he would undo her hobbles and set her free before nightfall because she would prefer to walk, rather than run. The weaver did as she asked and, curious, he followed her down the street. All over the village, elephants were trumpeting the same request, but the weaver was the only one who understood. The elephants knew trouble would come from the sea!

'The weaver informed his family and asked them to warn all their neighbours. He freed all the working elephants he could find. Then he returned, bone-weary, to complete his carpet. He tied the last thread as the ground began to shake – and waited, too tired to move, resigned to his fate.

'But when his family returned to their flooded village the next day, they found him asleep near his loom. Most of the village was destroyed – and those who had refused to heed the warning had died – but the wave had not reached the weaver's house. There is a very clear account of these events in the family records. He was honoured among the villagers for sounding the warning – and honoured among elephants for being a good listener.'

Madam Eleanor was now speaking so softly the children had to strain to hear. 'And the last person to weave an Invisible Creation was – my dear sister Nina. It is . . .' She did not need to finish her sentence. 'Our tiger rug,' whispered Lucy.

36
Family Dramas

Lucy's head was swimming. 'But Madam Eleanor, how do you fit in to all this? You don't even look like a real Telarian. And I thought Nina was Australian.' Perhaps it was rude, but she had to know.

'Our mother came from Ireland,' Madam Eleanor said, not seeming to mind. 'She was a glorious red-haired beauty, with eyes like a cat, and she married into one of the oldest families in Telares – a family of master weavers. They were famous for their work, and in spring and summer the family lived and wove their creations in one of the most beautiful parts of the island, in a house filled with the spirit of the sea. In autumn, they would return to Pasadena Square to draw new designs and run their extremely successful business.

'My father was delighted when my mother gave birth to triplets – three beautiful girls. But only after their birth did he tell her about the Carpet of All Creation – and the fate of her newborn girls' tragic ancestor.

'It was the custom for the skills of weaving to be passed

on to those who showed the talent and the love. Nina and I learned at Angel's age – but it was something we loved, not something we were chained up and forced to do. We still ran around like wild things much of the time, playing and exploring with the village children. In turn, I passed these weaving skills on to my daughter Sofia, and, when her own daughter, Angel, was big enough, we taught her together. She showed enormous passion and aptitude for one so young.

'Our triplet sister, Carlotta, however, hated weaving. She did not want to learn, but she was also jealous of our skills. It caused much friction as we were growing up. Still, we had an idyllic childhood. Our home was filled with laughter and the scent of the sea, and every day my relatives worked on their magnificent rugs, bringing much honour and prosperity to the family.

'When Nina married Theodore she moved to Australia. She missed our beautiful home in the jungle so much that she asked her husband to build her a copy.'

'The Mermaid House,' breathed Lucy.

'Yes,' said Madam Eleanor, 'and my childhood summer home, before the Bulls came and stole everything, was . . .'

'The other Mermaid House – the jungle jail!'

'Yes,' said Madam Eleanor heavily. 'When Nina left, I missed her terribly. Carlotta's jealousy had grown, along with her greed. She refused to do any kind of work herself and spent her whole time at parties – but expected the family to support her with our weaving. Then, she began to argue with us, insisting we abandon the old-fashioned ways and use modern machines to make more carpets and more money. She quarrelled badly with my father, who knew the old, slow ways made the finest carpets, and she too left Telares, and we did not hear from her for a long time.

'Nina was always kind-hearted. When too many years had passed, she searched for Carlotta and found her, of all places, on the neighbouring archipelago of Burchimo, where the Bulls came from! She had married a Bull soldier and was pregnant. We were horrified to learn he was beating her, and brave Nina helped her run away to Australia, where Carlotta's son Nigel was born.

'Carlotta and Nigel lived near Nina and she looked after them for years, showing nothing but kindness – until our parents died and Carlotta saw her chance. She came back to Telares and demanded the family open a factory and begin to sell the one kind of carpet we had always refused to – our Carpets of All Creation. Of course, we declined. We offered her money instead, which she took, but this time she never forgave us. We were estranged and none of us have ever seen her again, not even Nina. Even Nigel, her son, maintains he does not know where she is.

'After the Bulls invaded Telares, Nina rang with the ominous news that she had made an Invisible Creation. I knew what was required. I went back to our Mermaid House, where I did my best work, and began weaving immediately. But then,' her voice grew angry, 'the Bulls marched into the village and took everything. We had to flee back to Pasadena Square. I had to leave my precious carpet and my dragon chest. Thankfully,' she said with a grateful glance at Lucy and Ricardo, 'the Bull Commander does not have the key. However, what is inside is worth more than money. It is my half of the pattern of the Carpet of All Creation.'

'Your half?' asked Lucy.

'Yes, the pattern in Nina's chest looks like a complete pattern but, for security reasons, we always kept the halves separate. Nina was to secretly send me its partner when I had finished my half. Unfortunately, the Bull Commander took one look at the carpet I had begun to weave at the Mermaid House and recognised the most famous pattern in the world. He knew he could sell it for a fortune if only it could be completed. He began kidnapping children, thinking in his greed that their small fingers would make the finest work – not understanding that the best carpets are made with love. By sheer terrible coincidence, Angel was one of the kidnapped ones – he took her from her mother, my daughter Sofia, in the park.

'Yet the villagers were loyal to us. They told me Angel was imprisoned in my childhood home! I could not believe it. They also said the Commander had become desperate for the pattern. He had threatened the villagers, so I arranged for a fake pattern to be delivered to him and tore it in half to tantalise him.

'And that is where Nigel comes in. Of course, Carlotta had told him about the Carpets of All Creation. He has grown up with her hard, jealous heart and her hunger for riches. Worse, he has tracked down his family in Burchimo. That is understandable – a man needs to know who his father is – but Nigel is now loyal to the Bulls. He has struck a deal to sell them the pattern for the Carpet of All Creation. That is why he is desperate for Nina's dragon chest.'

At these words, Madam Eleanor smiled at Lucy and Ricardo.

'We must thank you for keeping the chest safe and for becoming involved in Angel's plight. And, as for you Telarian children, I cannot believe the risks you have taken. You have already been through so much and yet you still had the heart to help Angel. We can never repay you. To be separated from your loved ones is a terrible cruelty, especially when you are as young as Angel.'

She stroked the Tiger-cat on Angel's lap.

'But Angel and I did, of course, have other ways of staying in touch.'

She looked directly into Lucy's eyes.

'Lucia, Euphoria here picked you and your brother, and I suspect, your impressive puppy here, even before you had set foot in the Mermaid House in Kurrawong.'

'Oh!' was all Lucy could say.

'You see, the matter had become extremely urgent. Angel being kidnapped changed everything. Unbeknown to him, the Bull Commander had a member of the true line – one of the only people on the island who could create a genuine Carpet of All Creation. And Angel couldn't help herself. Her talent insisted she do her best. The carpet she wove with so many tears of homesickness has spoken directly to you all.'

Madam Eleanor met their eyes in turn.

'We are all in terrible danger, but you brave young people have faced that before – and,' she spoke with an air of mystery, 'you have not always been left to fend for yourselves alone. I trust that in the morning you will have the help you need to rescue your friend.'

She refused to explain any further and the children were too tired to insist. They fell gratefully into hastily made antique beds, knowing it would not be long before Eduardo tapped them on their shoulders, in the darkness just before dawn.

However, the touch that came first was from a different source. The Tiger-cat, who had kept a surprisingly low profile all evening, was suddenly full of skittish life. Lying awake, her mind buzzing with everything Madam Eleanor had said and conscious of a knot of nerves in her tummy about what was in store, Lucy watched, intrigued, as one by one, each child was honoured with a visit. The Tiger-cat gazed intently at each of them, even sparing a few minutes for two rather nervous monkeys and a dog who would purr if he could. Then she curled up on Lucy's bed and went to sleep.

37

Monkey Magic

The only warning the Bulls had was no warning at all: a ginger cat slipping down a cobblestone street in the old quarter of Telares City just before dawn. The Bull patrol on duty did not notice the feline padding past, but they could not help jumping a few minutes later at a terrific crash in the alley behind the Angelus Hospital. Half-asleep, the young soldiers jerked into action, bursting into the alley, guns at the ready. But what good are guns when your enemy is a heap of toppled-over dustbins, and the tail of the stray cat responsible for the evil-smelling chaos is already disappearing over the wall?

The soldiers had done their duty. Lucy was delighted to see them leaving the alley, holding their noses. What the soldiers failed to notice was six children, two monkeys and a dog slipping through the shadows at the other end of the alley, through a delivery gate and into the grounds of the hospital.

The hospital was a sprawling old building, three storeys high, surrounded by gardens and a high stone wall. As elsewhere in Telares, the air was heavy and sweet with the scent of mangoes. Staring at the back of the building from the shadows of an enormous tree, Lucy gave silent thanks for Madam Eleanor's flying fingers.

'Much too easy,' the old woman had sighed as the hospital's security system yielded its secrets. Rahel's face had lit up, then she'd become a stern schoolmarm, making them all, even the little ones, memorise a plan of the hospital, its entrances and exits and, most importantly of all, the location of Room 3-15. Now, gazing up at the window of Carlos' room, Lucy wished that 3 stood for something other than the third storey. A dim light burned in the room but the children could see nothing.

'What if he's not there?' Ricardo piped up helpfully.

'He will be,' said Lucy with a confidence she didn't feel, examining with a sinking heart the network of drainage pipes that crawled over the wall. At least the Bulls had hidden him away at the back of the building, where it was quieter.

'You'd have to be a monkey to get up there,' she whispered to Rahel.

'A monkey,' Rahel repeated thoughtfully.

As one, the two girls turned to their little brothers.

'Do you think . . . ?'

The boys didn't have to be asked twice.

'Give me the note,' hissed Pablo. He twisted the scrap of paper into a scarf and gently tied it around Toro's monkey's neck, making him look like a little bandit.

'OK, send 'em up, but be careful.'

Far too cheerfully, Ricardo and Toro trotted across the expanse of lawn that separated their sheltering tree from the hospital wall, monkeys clinging to their backs. Lucy held her breath. Phew, they had reached the shadows of the wall. But what if the monkeys refused to climb? All the flaws in their strategy were suddenly very obvious to her. How do you make a monkey climb a wall if it doesn't want to? It was a few seconds before she realised the boys had no intention of being separated from their soulmates. Like a pair of humpbacked twins, first Toro and then Ricardo leaped with unexpected agility at the drainpipe that criss-crossed the brickwork of the building. Quick as lightning they scaled the first storey before their big sisters knew what was happening. They took a brief rest on a window awning and turned to wave cheerily.

'Why, you little . . .' Lucy hissed, but Rahel hushed her with a hand on the arm. Then the boys were scaling the second storey with preternatural skill. Lucy turned to Rahel open-mouthed.

'What the . . . ?'

But a slow smile had dawned on the Telarian girl's face. 'A monkey,' she said warmly, and suddenly Lucy understood there had to be certain advantages to spending all your time with a monkey clinging to your neck. And it wasn't half as creepy as having a snake crawl over your foot.

With dawning appreciation Lucy turned to watch the boys perch on another window awning, so high it made her feel dizzy, then turn back for the final assault. In seconds they were clinging to the ivy under the window where Carlos was supposed to be. And that's when the brown uniformed figure appeared silhouetted against the light.

Everyone froze. The monkey brothers seemed to disappear flat against the wall. There was a scratch and a flare. The Bull soldier lit a cigarette and leaned his elbows on the windowsill. For interminable minutes he looked out into the garden, calmly smoking. Each time he leaned out to ash his cigarette Lucy saw a humpbacked shape shudder involuntarily below him.

'Please don't fall,' she tried to pray. She felt like vomiting. He must have ashed his cigarette about fifteen times, and Lucy's prayer became a direct appeal to whichever monkey was copping the ash shower: 'Please don't screech.'

They didn't. After an excruciating final drag on his cigarette, the soldier tossed it into the garden, yawned, scratched himself, turned his back on the window and walked away.

Awfully slow minutes passed, then one of the boys swung up the last stretch of ivy and craned his head carefully over the window. In a flash he was inside, followed instantly by his friend.

Compared to what had just transpired, everything then happened ridiculously quickly. In seconds both boys climbed back out of the window, shimmied down the wall and streaked back across the lawns to their sweating big sisters.

'Well done!' Lucy breathed.

'Is he . . . ?' Rahel could not finish the question.

'They shot him in the leg,' Ricardo said, far too happily.

'And they're not feeding him enough, 'cause he ate the note,' offered Toro.

There was a snort of laughter from Janella, quickly smothered, and then Pablo's quiet voice asked, 'But where's my scarf?'

Ricardo and Toro pointed at each other. 'He's got it.'

Personal jinx.

38

Trashcan Trap

Any thoughts these monkeys may have harboured of shinning back up the wall were dashed by the appearance of not one but two Bull soldiers at the window. Barely breathing, the children melted as far back into the shadows of the mango trees as they could. Then, of course, came the shout they had been dreading. They heard an exclamation of surprise in Burchimese and one of the soldiers strode past the window, clutching Pablo's scarf in his hand.

'D'oh,' was all Ricardo had to offer.

Without further discussion, the group crept backwards along the wall of the garden and into the alley. Heart pounding, Lucy looked anxiously about. She knelt on the ground and listened with her palms.

'Patrol! Coming this way. We've only got a few minutes.'

No one argued. They trotted stealthily up the alley, away from the approaching soldiers, but soon found their path blocked by a pile of upturned garbage cans. Trying to move them could be fatally noisy. They would have to squeeze past, but that was going to be noisy too.

'Just what we needed,' scowled Lucy, but an insistent miaow above caught her attention. The alley followed the high wall of the hospital. Perched on the brickwork was the Tiger-cat, tail lashing.

It was Rahel's turn to fall to her knees. 'Another patrol. Coming from this end. We're trapped!'

The Tiger-cat hissed urgently.

'We've got to go over the wall,' snapped Lucy.

'But that will take us back into the hospital and they're bound to be looking for us.' This Pablo said with a disgusted look at the monkey-handlers.

'They're looking for us out here,' said Lucy, exasperated. 'And they don't know how the scarf got there. They'll be thinking only a monkey could climb that wall. And if they do think there was a break-in, they probably think we've gone. The last thing they'll expect is for us to break back in.'

'Hush, I am detecting something unusual approaching. I do not believe it is human.' Rahel concentrated, frowning, and then raised her head in alarm. 'Army horses!'

In a few seconds, they all heard a distinctive clip-clop, clip-clop coming from one end of the alley – horses at a fast trot, heading their way. Only Janella looked remotely pleased and a strange, faraway, listening look settled on her face. But Rahel was not waiting for the horse-lover, or for Lucy and Pablo to resolve their differences. She went crazy instead.

Crash! The Telarian rolled an enormous garbage can in one direction down the alley with a horrific clatter. She grabbed a second and sent it in the other direction.

'What are you doing!!!!???' yelped Lucy. More garbage

cans joined the others and then, 'Let's go!' was all Rahel said, levering herself up on a third bin and disappearing over the wall to the purring appreciation of the Tiger-cat. The monkey boys disappeared after her before Lucy knew what was happening. Janella snapped out of her reverie and followed, but paused on the top of the wall to cast a longing look up the alley, as the sound of trotting hooves grew closer. As if in reply, a horse whickered off in the darkness.

Lucy scaled the wall, only to freeze at a desperate howl from T-Tongue. She shot a mute appeal at Pablo and he gathered the enormous puppy in his arms and passed him, struggling and whimpering, up to Lucy. She pushed him unceremoniously off the other side and jumped herself, Pablo landing heavily beside her. Above her head, Lucy could still hear the Tiger-cat purring. On the other side of the wall sounded quick-marching feet and the clip-clop of a horse, terribly close, plus shouted orders in Burchimese and a clang and crash as both groups of soldiers met a rolling barricade of rubbish bins in the alley.

The Tiger-cat yowled provocatively and Lucy heard one of the soldiers swear, she was sure, even without under-standing Burchimese. She could hear hurried conference, laughter and then a stone hitting the wall where the Tiger-cat had been only seconds before. Now, that furry body was rubbing about Lucy's legs. The soldiers marched off in both directions, talking loudly. Clearly, they thought it had all been a false alarm. Round two to the Tiger-cat.

A horse neighed right on the other side of the wall and Lucy had to grab Janella's hand to stop her climbing back over again. More swearing in Burchimese, the snap of a crop stinging horseflesh and a snort of equine fury – but finally the horse obeyed its impatient rider and trotted away up the alley after the soldiers.

'I'm going to kill them,' hissed Janella. Lucy stared at her, uncomprehending, wondering what on earth had got into her normally peace-loving friend.

39

The Rescue

Dragging Janella away from the wall, Lucy suddenly could see where she was. This was both good and bad. Good, because she saw that by jumping back over the wall at that particular spot they had, by luck, landed in a dense section of garden at the front of the hospital which offered plenty of cover. Bad, because the reason she could see better was the oyster-pink glow of the rising sun – dawn. Carlos' deadline.

The ornate entrance gates stood off to her right, closed and barred. From them, a driveway swept up to the steps of the hospital. Only a few metres of open space separated the children's hiding place from the steps.

Janella tried to stand up at the clip-clop of an approaching horse. Horse or horses? It seemed terribly loud for just one. Again Lucy had to pull her down into cover.

Then came the urgent roar of a car. It screeched to a halt beyond the gate and a harsh voice shouted an order. Bolts slid free with a clang and clunk and the heavy gates groaned open. A military van sped up the driveway to the hospital and two guards in the rag-tag uniform of the militia jumped out and ran up the stairs to pound on the heavy wooden doors. A third, wearing the smarter brown uniform, swung casually out and, leaning against the van, lit a cigarette. The Bull Commander, looking so much more relaxed than when Lucy had last seen him, was taking a special interest indeed in his prisoner of special interest!

Clip-clop, several soldiers on horseback trotted through the gates, and again Lucy had to grab Janella's hand. She was rigid with tension. What had got into her? The riders formed a tight guard around the car, making way only when the two guards appeared again in the open doorway bearing a stretcher with a familiar dark head on its pillow. One of the guards had a bright scarf wrapped about his wrist, causing Pablo to take an angry breath.

A man wearing a white coat and a stethoscope accompanied the stretcher. He was clearly distressed. Lucy could not understand the conversation that followed but the doctor seemed to be remonstrating with the Bull Commander. But the Commander calmly finished his cigarette, stepped up close to the doctor and – flicked the butt in his face. The doctor flinched and turned away, head lowered.

The Commander issued a curt order and the stretcher-bearers moved to the back of the van. In seconds Carlos would be inside, the doors would close and the van would roar away. And that would be that.

The tingle in Lucy's feet became a sizzle, then a simmer. Her eyes locked on the back of the Bull Commander's head. Her chest began to bubble. She dimly registered Janella wriggling free of her restraining hand and taking a step through the garden, making an eerie whickering sound as she did so. Another step and the whicker grew to a moan. One more, and she had left the sheltering trees. That got Lucy's full attention. Janella was pacing openly up the driveway, wailing low in her throat like a madwoman. But the soldiers on horseback did not notice, they were too busy trying to control their suddenly uncontrollable mounts. The disciplined, highly trained military horses that had trotted up the drive a few minutes ago were rearing and bucking. The largest, a huge black stallion with a star on his forehead, screamed a terrible challenge to the sky and Lucy saw the panic on his rider's face.

The Bull Commander swung to see Janella marching in that weird hypnotised gait up the drive and issued a sharp command to the stretcher-bearers. They quickly tried to load the stretcher into the back of the van, but Janella's voice found a new unearthly pitch and, as one, the horses plunged into a sweating frenzy. The black stallion reared, bucked violently and threw his rider off. He lay in a crumpled heap and the stallion charged towards the van. The other horses screamed defiance, dislodged their riders and followed.

At the same time the apparently comatose figure of Carlos burst into action. He threw himself off the stretcher, dragging his injured leg behind him, and rolled under the van. Taken by surprise, the stretcher-bearers tripped and by the time they found their feet the stallion was almost upon them. They cowered and screamed as it reared over them.

The Bull Commander drew his gun and aimed at the stallion's mighty chest. Janella spun about to face Lucy.

Her face was lit with a strange concentration and her unearthly song sang right to Lucy's heart. Their silent communication took but a second – not that Lucy needed telling: Janella was begging her to save the stallion. The bubbling in her chest was now a rolling boil. Lucy locked eyes again on the Commander and unleashed a mighty roar. The Commander took his eyes off the rearing, screaming stallion and found himself trapped in the spotlight of Lucy's protective rage.

Lucy was aware of Rahel materialising at her side and when her hand gripped Lucy's it was as though 240 volts of pure power passed between them. Suddenly, they had all the time in the world. The rotation of the planet itself seemed to slow down to the pace of their padding feet, crunching in tandem across the gravel drive to where the Commander stood rooted in the spotlight of their combined lethal gaze.

Lucy was dimly aware of some commotion to the side of her, then Ricardo and Toro flew past, golden monkeys screeching in unholy glee. Another hand grasped her free one and she did not have to turn to know that Pablo had stepped up. Again there was that exchange of electric anger and the three of them bore down on the shivering Commander.

When it came, the attack was bloodless. A mighty growl overtook Lucy and then she was leaping, teeth and claws bared for the man who held Carlos' life in the palm of his hand. She was hungrily aware of a pack of tawny, striped hunters, small and large, close by and she growled with a jealous fury. She would tear his throat out! She!

The horses, finally sent insane with an ancient fear of

the feline, screamed and galloped in a foaming sweat for the gate. Janella screamed with them and somehow her distress got through to Lucy. She fought for self control – and won! She came back into her body, and found herself crouched over the Commander, snarling. She held his terrified eyes, knowing her tiger self could kill him, but her human self would not. She smiled, and he fainted dead away. Lucy rocked back on her heels and saw Rahel and Pablo kneeling on either side of her, stunned and shaking their heads as though they had both walked into the same bus. And there was the Tiger-cat. No! Two Tiger-cats! But before Lucy's awestruck gaze the golden eyes of one morphed into the black eyes of – Angel!

'Angel! What are you doing here?' But the little girl grinned and melted away with the other Tiger-cat into the garden.

The black stallion, covered in white foam, stamped restlessly nearby. Lucy saw Janella walk slowly towards the huge beast, speaking gently. Gradually, it settled and let her stroke its nose. Janella made a low, keening sound and the stallion whickered in response. An answering neigh came from the street and, one by one, the other three riderless horses trotted back through the gates. They tossed their heads nervously but Janella gradually soothed them, and took their reins.

Then she climbed athletically up into the saddle of the black stallion as though she had been doing it all her life. Which would have been fine, except Lucy was fairly certain that the only thing Janella had ever ridden was a camel at the school fete – and she didn't think that counted.

Lucy turned at a simian screech. The two stretcher-bearers had crawled to the stairs and lay, helpless, trying to shelter as best they could from a storm of mangoes raining down from the tree that arched over the roof of the hospital's front verandah. On the ground, two monkeys called Ricardo and Toro had grabbed the guards' weapons. That snapped Lucy out of her altered state.

'Oh no you don't,' she hissed and leaped to her feet. She strode over to the boys and grabbed the guns from their hands. A shadow materialised and put a hand on her elbow. She jumped. Eduardo, holding tightly to Angel's hand, gently took the guns from her. He slipped them inside his voluminous ninja suit and padded quietly towards the white-coated doctor, still standing on the steps of the hospital, his eyes huge. Casually Eduardo let the sleeve of his black ninja suit ride up and Lucy clearly saw the tiger tattooed on his forearm – and the doctor saw it too. The doctor held Eduardo's gaze for a long moment, and nodded.

'*Thank you*,' said Eduardo, and turned to the stretcher-bearers. He held up a commanding hand to the monkeys and, miraculously, the storm of mangoes ceased. Eduardo knelt near one of the stretcher-bearers and held out his hand mutely. Without complaint the militiaman handed him a set of keys.

'And I will take that,' Pablo said, snatching his scarf from the other guard's hand. But the guard did not seem to notice. Instead he was gazing at Lucy as though she were a she-devil. He had given her the very same look not so long ago, but very, very far away. It was the militiaman who had witnessed the tiger scene at Nigel Scar-Skull's warehouse in Kurrawong! There was no doubt. He must have caught the first flight home. Bad move.

But the doctor gestured urgently towards the van. Carlos was trying to haul himself out from underneath. Lucy rushed to his side.

'Are you OK?'

It was a stupid question. He was horribly pale and the bandages on his leg were soaked in blood. He smiled weakly. 'Many thanks for the note. But couldn't you have given me a bit more information? "Be ready." What did that mean?' His grin took the sting out of his words.

Lucy smiled back and swept her hand to indicate the wild scene about them.

'Well, we wanted to warn you about wild horses and Janella going nuts, and Angel turning into a Tiger-cat again, and I think Pablo and Rahel might have learned how to become tigers, and a few other things . . . but we weren't sure if you were in the mood for reading.'

Carlos tried to answer but suddenly his head fell back on the gravel and the doctor was immediately by his side, a needle in his hand.

'He is too weak and he is in pain,' he said urgently. 'He needs sleep and antibiotics.' He tossed Lucy a box of pills and expertly slipped the needle into Carlos' thigh. Then Eduardo picked up the teenager as though he were nothing but a teddy bear and placed him gently on the stretcher. Carlos' eyes were closed before Eduardo and the doctor had lifted the stretcher.

'Where are you taking him?' begged Lucy, feeling bereft. After those awful hours on the river, when she

221

feared Carlos was dead, it was too hard to have him taken away again so soon, even if that was what was best for him.

'He needs care. A rebel hospital is the only way he will get it. There is a secret one on the other side of the city,' Eduardo said with rough kindness.

Lucy nodded reluctant agreement and handed Eduardo the antibiotics. But as Eduardo and the doctor loaded the stretcher into the van there was a sudden disturbance. Eduardo emerged from the vehicle, struggling with a man in an extremely loud shirt. The giant Telarian had the upper hand quickly, wrapping him in a bear-hug.

'Leave me alone. My embassy will hear of this. I'm an important man, I tell you,' Nigel squeaked uselessly. Then the important man caught sight of Lucy, Ricardo and T-Tongue and seemed to stop breathing for a minute.

'I saw what you did to my brother,' Nigel Scar-Skull gasped. 'It's not normal. You're a freak! You ought to be locked up. And those feral animals should be shot.'

Eduardo threw Nigel expertly over his shoulder like a protesting child as the doctor emerged with another stretcher. Nigel was strapped in it with much complaint and could only watch when Eduardo sprang back into the van and appeared holding a dragon chest as though it weighed as much as a shoebox. It was too much for Nigel, who shouted, 'Get your dirty hand off my brother's chest.'

Lucy took a step towards him, a growl simmering, but the scream of a siren distracted her.

'Go!' the doctor urged. Eduardo nodded.

'Now!' he ordered.

'But what about him?' Lucy said, gesturing at the struggling Nigel.

'I'll take care of him,' said Eduardo, lifting the stretcher without any help, causing Nigel to struggle even harder.

'And that?' she asked, gesturing at the chest.

'I believe I know who owns it.' Eduardo smiled and put it back inside the van. He slammed the door on Carlos, Nigel and the chest and ran to the driver's seat as the sirens grew louder.

'The soldiers will follow the van. Go in the opposite direction. And don't worry about your friend. I will lose the soldiers,' he promised.

The doctor ran back up the stairs and the big hospital doors slammed behind him, as the van screamed out the gates. The sirens grew louder and the children ran for the trees.

'The guards who lost their horses, they have raised the alarm,' Rahel panted. The sirens were making the four horses plunge again, so Janella, astride the black stallion, crooned quietly until they settled.

'My horses aren't going back into the Bull army,' she announced.

'My' horses? What had got into her?

'C'mon,' Janella urged, dangling a set of reins at Lucy.

Lucy grabbed Ricardo's hand, ran to a big brown horse, vaulted up and dragged her brother up behind her. Rahel did the same, hauling Toro onto a grey horse. Pablo didn't need to be told and was already aboard a glorious chestnut. Janella's stallion reared up one more time, gave a commanding neigh to the other horses and cantered off through the gardens towards the back of the hospital.

As the first military vehicles screamed into the front driveway of the hospital, four horses and a dog were galloping out through the back gate. By the time the sun burst into the sky they had disappeared up the alley and were charging towards the harbour.

40

Going Home

The horses clattered across the bridge towards the southern side of the harbour where the children had met Madam Eleanor.

'Where are we going?' shouted Lucy to Rahel.

'We will have to go back the way we came and then swim the horses up the River of Souls. Pablo knows a way to lead the horses in closer to the tunnel entrance.'

'Good!' said Lucy, 'we've got to get home. Any longer and Mum'll be wondering where we are.'

'And we must get back to the rebel base,' said Rahel. 'Larissa will be filled with worry – and fury. We have caused a lot of trouble.'

The horses swung left off the bridge and raced along the beach lined with jetties and boats. Janella turned at one point and shouted, 'Hurry, the stallion thinks we are being pursued.' Without needing to be asked, the horses found another gear and their powerful strides ate up the distance. Soon they had passed the jetty where Madam Eleanor's houseboat had been moored. Lucy couldn't resist a lingering look across the river towards where she knew the mysterious old house was, but could not make it out. Then her horse was flying into the forest and all she could see was the powerful haunches and tail of Janella's horse, still leading the way.

The black stallion seemed not to need directions from Pablo but stormed on through the early sunlight. They charged past where Lucy and Ricardo had stumbled out of the water and on, through dense forest where the track was barely visible.

Finally Janella's stallion pulled up before a rocky outcrop near the river. Peering through the trees, Lucy realised they were very close to where the River of Souls plunged out of the mountain cavern. Blowing and snorting, the horses stood as though waiting for something. In a minute a limp, exhausted, panting form stumbled up the track after them.

'T-Tongue!' Lucy called, suddenly overwhelmed with emotion. 'Good boy. I'm sorry, we should have given you a lift.'

She alighted, wrapped the puppy in her ninja coat and mounted again, settling him before her on the saddle.

'Let's go,' Pablo said, and at a nod from Janella he moved his horse into the lead. He rounded the rocky outcrop and Lucy noticed a gap in the rocks like a door.

'Welcome back to the River of Souls,' he said proudly and led the party through the narrow entrance. The sandy floor immediately sloped down and soon Lucy could smell fresh water. The horses whickered in excitement and it was not long before their shoes clattered on a rocky beach and they dipped grateful muzzles in the river. The strange grey twilight of the river cavern engulfed the children once again.

'We must hurry,' said Rahel anxiously, looking towards the other side of the river. 'The Bulls may come back this way. They know this is where it all began.'

Janella urged her stallion into the river and they began the long swim back up to the entrance to the Kurrawong tunnel. Luckily, the tide was in their favour. It would have been impossible otherwise.

'Why are you going this way?' Lucy suddenly thought to ask Rahel. 'You could just ride to the rebel base from here.'

Her friend looked strangely at her. 'I could not let you leave without an escort,' she scolded.

Lucy shook her head as though she were dealing with a madwoman.

A tired silence descended. Only the gentle slosh of the swimming horses and their steady breathing intervened. Then Pablo made an exclamation of recognition. 'There, you see the paintings. We are almost there.'

As the fairy lights of the grottos drew near, Lucy looked nervously across to the other side of the river where, just yesterday, Bull soldiers had been shooting at them.

When Pablo urged his horse towards the steps that marked the tunnel back to Kurrawong, their relief was overwhelming.

41

Another Goodbye

Janella sang the frightened horses through the tunnel – that was the only way Lucy could describe it. As they clattered into the void, the black stallion began to skitter and paw the rocky ground. But Janella sang a wordless floating melody that seemed to settle the great beast. He stopped jerking on his reins and stood calmly and then allowed Janella to lead him deeper into the tunnel. Lucy and Rahel walked ahead of Janella, bat senses stretched, to guide them. The others followed, taking it in turns to lead the horses. T-Tongue was a very good boy and stayed out of reach of the horses' hooves.

It was much harder going up than coming down. The steep climb exhausted the already tired smaller kids, but Janella would not let anyone ride. 'It's not fair on the horses,' she said. Finally they reached the fork in the tunnel and turned right, back to Telares.

'You do not have to escort us,' said Rahel.

'Yes, we do,' said Lucy firmly.

When they reached the entrance to Telares, the curtain

of greenery was already open and soft sunlight fell onto the sandy floor of the tunnel. Lucy spied the Tiger-cat sitting in a tree, which she decided showed great sensitivity to the horses.

Rahel and Pablo mounted and Lucy hoisted Toro and monkey up to his big sister. Then she turned to Ricardo, ready for a fight. It was unnecessary. Ricardo was already explaining the situation to his own golden charge.

'It's like this, little bro,' he said. 'Mum has never met you, so it's not that she doesn't like you, but if she did meet you, she . . . wouldn't like you. And that Nigel guy might shoot you. So you'd better go with Toro.' At that, he bravely handed his little furry friend up to Toro, who had tucked his own monkey gently into a saddlebag. Ricardo's monkey snuggled in next to the other golden head – and fell asleep. But Ricardo wasn't looking. He had walked back into the tunnel without a backward glance, shoulders just a little hunched.

'We must depart,' said Rahel, without much enthusiasm.

'Are you really going to cop it when you get back to the base?' asked Lucy.

'Indeed,' Rahel and Pablo said together in exactly the same tone of doom. Then they both laughed.

'But it was worth it,' Rahel declared, 'to see Angel back with her grandparents.'

'And to roar at the Commander – again,' chortled Lucy.

'And to see the River of Souls,' said Pablo, grinning.

'And to meet the horses,' said you-know-who.

Then everyone grew pensive.

'I hope Carlos is OK,' said Lucy, voicing everyone's fears.

'He will be,' said Rahel strongly. 'The rebel doctors are the best!'

'And Eduardo is awesome!' said Ricardo, who had composed himself and emerged from the tunnel.

'Indeed,' said Toro.

'But,' mused Lucy, 'we've still got some work to do. We have to get the carpet back. And what was all that Nigel was saying about his brother owning the dragon chest? You don't think . . . ?'

Then all the pieces fell into place for Lucy. The Bull Commander was Nigel's brother! She didn't quite understand how or why, but she knew they had a family business – slavery.

Well, not if she had anything to do with it.

'Never fear,' said Rahel, reading her face. 'I will tell Larissa everything we have learned about this Nigel character and she will not be so furious with me. She may even believe me when I describe Eduardo to her. I am sure he is a famous rebel. And perhaps she will let me out again in a few weeks. Say, at the next full moon?'

'I'll be here at the next full moon,' said Lucy, holding her gaze.

'And I'll be here because you guys will have to take two extra horses home with you today. They won't be able to jump out of the pit at Lucy's place so I'll be back to make sure you're treating them right,' Janella said severely, then gave a mischievous smile.

Lucy hadn't thought of the pit. She had just imagined the horses grazing happily up in the clearing above her house, drinking from the cool mountain stream.

Disappointed, she passed her reins to Rahel. Janella handed the black stallion's reins to Pablo.

'Just sing to him if he gets jumpy,' she said casually and Pablo began to look worried.

'And I'll be here to practise shrieking like my monkey,' said Ricardo cheerfully, which made Lucy decide it was a good time to leave. They moved back towards the tunnel and turned to wave as the Telarians galloped off into the jungle.

There was no galloping from any of the Kurrawong kids – that trudge through the tunnel was the longest of Lucy's life. They spoke not a word until, deep in the cavernous darkness, something leathery and furry brushed against Janella's face. Even then she was too tired to scream. She just said, 'Hi Batman!' and soldiered on. When they finally clambered out of the pit, groaning, they realised they had to lug all the camping gear back or it just wouldn't look right and Mum would get suspicious. They were almost dead on their feet by the time they hit the kitchen. Mum and Grandma were both there and Mum began accusing them of not getting enough sleep and Grandma said they also were not eating enough. They pleaded guilty to both charges, ate a hearty meal and fell asleep.

Hours later Lucy awoke to Mum's raised voice.

'Mr Adams, I don't what or how much jungle juice you have been consuming in whatever country you are in, but I am telling you both my children are asleep in their beds. They have not left the country in their entire lives. They don't even have passports. So I fail to see how they could have become illegal immigrants overnight, in a country I haven't even heard of, let alone stolen horses from armed soldiers. Perhaps, when you fly back to Australia, you should see a doctor. Goodnight.'

Smiling sweetly, Lucy fell asleep to the Tiger-cat's satisfied purring.

42

Nigel's Undoing

The following few days passed in a sleepy blur of marble cake and movies. Then, on Friday morning, T-Tongue's frantic barking drew Lucy out onto the verandah to stand open-mouthed at the posse of strange cars that had just pulled up. When the TV news van with its big satellite dish on the roof rushed up, she became a little worried, guilty memories of their warehouse adventure last Saturday night flooding back. When Nigel's car with its vote-for-me sign arrived, she knew they were really in trouble.

'Janella, Ricardo, look at this.'

But Mum and Grandma, of course, got there first.

'What's going on?'

'I don't know, but I'm sick of that loony. He's the one who phoned me in the middle of the night, ranting and raving, accusing my kids of crazy things. I'm going to find out what he's up to,' said Mum, marching down the stairs towards Nigel Scar-Skull, who had stepped out of his car wearing a dark suit and a very sad face.

'Excuse me,' said Mum. 'If you're here to examine my

children's passports, I told you, they don't have any. And would you please tell me why this crowd is outside my home?'

'I am here for my aunt's memorial service,' Nigel said, pompously. 'I would ask you to show some respect.' Then he marched off towards the television cameras.

'Well, you could have let me know—' Mum stopped, as two men in black carried a long table through the front gate.

'What are you doing?' she demanded, following them back into the garden.

'Getting ready for the priest,' one said, as though she were stupid. They put the table under a shady tree and began shaking out a long white tablecloth.

Mum shook her head, stunned, and Nigel gave her a particularly nasty triumphant glance as he walked past, a crowd of reporters at his heels. But he seemed to pale a little and began rubbing his head when he caught sight of Lucy and the others on the verandah. He looked away quickly.

'Where's the priest?' he snapped to the men at the table. As if on cue, a priest glided through the gate in full religious robes. Nigel straightened his tie and cleared his throat. A reporter shoved a radio microphone in Nigel's face, a camera flashed and the TV crew pushed closer.

'Look!' said Janella, 'It's Carla, from the *Kurrawong Crier*.'

Lucy saw a young woman jump out of a car that had just pulled up, smile excitedly when she saw Janella on the verandah and wave a newspaper at her. The kids streaked down the stairs, unable to contain their curiosity any longer.

'Thank you everyone for coming this morning,' Nigel

was saying, 'to support me in this very sad moment. My dear aunt, Nina Hawthorne, helped care for me when I was a child, and when her physical and mental health failed I had the privilege of caring for her in turn. Sadly, we are here to say our final farewells . . .'

But he never got any further.

'That,' said a familiar voice, 'would appear to be a trifle premature.'

The crowd of reporters turned as a dignified old lady with long white plaits, wearing fetching cat's-eye sunglasses, stepped through the gate, supported on the arm of a stout woman, who was squeezed into an eye-catching tiger-striped skirt and jacket.

'Hello, nephew,' said Nina Hawthorne, 'I trust your health is better than you clearly think mine is.'

The stout woman, who Lucy had last seen wearing the blue uniform and red cardigan of the matron of the Little Flower Nursing Home, where Lucy had first met Nina, waved breezily at Nigel. 'As you can see, your aunt has been under the best of care.'

The reporters swung back to Nigel, who gaped and turned a peculiar shade of lavender. Carla, Janella's sister's friend, jumped in first.

'Mr Adams – could you respond to the allegations, reported on the front page of today's *Crier*, that an international human rights group is investigating you for selling soccer balls and carpets made by child slaves?'

But Mr Adams could not respond to that, or any other question. A distinctive ginger cat had leaped up on the white tablecloth – and the man who wanted to be Mayor of Kurrawong had leaped into the nearest tree.

43

The Document

That night, Lucy's household watched the news with more enthusiasm than usual. The TV station must have thought the morning's events were pretty exciting too, because it kept running replays of Nigel climbing the tree, with the words *Candidate Scared of Cat* scrolling across the screen. But the big news, of course, was that Nina was alive. It led the bulletin. 'The elderly aunt of Kurrawong mayoral candidate Nigel Adams today attended her own funeral.' Then the camera stayed for a very long time on Nigel's face when he first caught sight of his long-lost aunt – and he didn't look at all happy to see her.

There was also an interview with Nina about why she had no intention of allowing the Mermaid House to be knocked down, and why the rainforest on the escarpment was far too fragile and wonderful to have buildings everywhere. But the old lady refused to say why she had hidden for so long, other than to hint at mysterious 'family reasons'. When Nigel finally climbed down from the tree, he kept saying how delighted he was that his aunt was safe and well, but anyone could see he was lying. When the reporters asked him how he felt about Nina hating his plans for the Mermaid House, he went very red in the face. And when Carla Kowalski asked him about slavery and Ten Star Jumbo balls he looked as if he wanted to climb back up the tree again. It was great.

What wasn't so great was Mum asking a whole lot of questions afterwards about why old Mrs Hawthorne was so pleased to see Lucy and Ricardo. Nina had come up and given them both a great big hug, and then given Janella and T-Tongue one each for good measure. So did Blue Uniform. When they both hugged Mum, she looked very confused. And then they hugged Grandma. And the TV cameras filmed it all!

'Why did Mrs Hawthorne keep thanking you so much?' Mum asked suspiciously, about fifty times.

'Oh, you know. Remember how we visited her in the nursing home in the Christmas holidays,' Lucy said weakly. Mum didn't look at all satisfied, but Grandma told her she should just get used to the idea that she had wonderful children.

'Really wonderful!' agreed Lucy and Ricardo.

However, Lucy was very relieved the next morning that both Mum and Grandma had gone off to vote (not for Nigel!) when Nina and Blue Uniform arrived again. They looked very pleased with themselves. Nina had unravelled her plaits and her long white hair crinkled all the way past her waist. She wore a T-shirt that read *Telares Forever* and carried three bunches of tiger lilies – one for each of the kids. Blue Uniform was draped in a startling tiger-print cape and carried a copy of the *Crier*. Lucy was secretly still a little scared of Blue Uniform, even if she did appear to be Nina's best friend, but the matron gave the kids a warm smile and, with a grand flourish, showed them the front page. There was a huge picture of Nina at her own funeral, and an even huger picture of Nigel up the tree. And there was a big headline that read '*Mayoral Candidate Refuses to Answer Questions about Slavery*' and another article inside about child labour in Telares. Carla had really gone for it.

Nina had tears in her eyes. 'You children are extraordinary,' she declared.

'But we lost the rug from the jungle jail!' burst out Lucy. 'And I lost your key to the dragon chest – but then we got it back. And Angel got lost – but we got her back too. And we got Madam Eleanor's chest back from the Bull Commander. But we didn't have time to get the rug back, and now Nigel's got it.' Lucy was despondent.

'But,' she continued more brightly, 'we're going to find it. If Nigel brought it here, we'll find it and take it back to Madam Eleanor. And if he didn't, we'll find it wherever he hid it in Telares. We lost it, so we'll find it.'

'You must,' Nina said seriously. 'I take it my sister Eleanor has explained its significance?'

'We know about the Carpets of All Creation,' Lucy said. 'I promise we'll get it back for you.' Janella and Ricardo nodded enthusiastically, and began going on about how they had to go back to Telares anyway to see horses and monkeys. Lucy seized her chance and raced to her bedroom. She returned with the envelope she had taken from the warehouse.

'Nina, Nigel says the Bull Commander is his brother.'

'His half-brother, actually,' said Nina. 'They share a Bull soldier for a father.'

'Oh,' said Lucy. 'Well, anyway, we found this in Nigel's safe,' she went on, a little guiltily. 'I've got a feeling it's important.'

'In that case, you must open it,' said Nina, with a twinkle in her ginger eyes.

Heart pounding, Lucy opened the envelope and removed a thick document.

'*Ten Star Jumbo Pty Ltd Profit Forecast*,' she read out loud, not really knowing what that meant. There was so much typing on the first few pages that she didn't bother reading them, but she paid attention when she came to a big map of Telares. It was covered with about twenty red dots and had a big headline that read *East Burchimo Profits*. Each dot had a name next to it, and a dollar sign – and each dollar sign was next to more money than Lucy could even imagine spending.

'I think it is a map of all the Ten Star Jumbo factories in Telares,' she whispered. 'Where all the Telarians are held prisoner!' She thought of Pablo and Rahel, and their desperate hope of seeing their families again. Their parents were at one of those red dots!

'May I see?' Nina politely requested. She read avidly. 'You are correct, Lucy,' she said. 'We must pass this on to the rebels immediately. They will be very happy to receive it.' Her eye travelled swiftly down the document. 'These papers could make all the difference to our cause. It not only lists the camps, but it shows how Nigel pays for the balls and carpets,' she said excitedly.

Lucy and Janella read over her shoulder.

'See? General this and Major that – and there's the Bull Commander, himself. And what's this? Bank Burchimo?'

'What!'

Nina's voice was hushed.

'It's a full list of bank accounts. If I am not mistaken, you children have stumbled on the money trail!'

'I want a money trail!' said Ricardo, and even though Lucy wasn't sure she entirely understood what a money trail was, she knew what to say to her little brother. 'Shut up, Ricardo!'

Somehow, she thought Rahel would know exactly what a money trail was – and so would Carla.

'Mmm, a money trail sounds good,' she said cheerfully, 'but what are we going to do if a tsunami comes?'

Nina grew very thoughtful. 'It is time for me to return to Telares after all these years to help my sister complete the Carpet of All Creation. You children must find it for us. If the old legends are true, it is the only thing we can do to avert disaster.'

'Now, Mrs Hawthorne, you know I'm not convinced by all this prophecy nonsense,' said Blue Uniform stoutly, 'but if a tsunami does strike, the island will need trained nurses – so I'll be coming with you.'

'See you there,' said Lucy, Ricardo and Janella together.

And, purring loudly enough to be heard in Telares, the Tiger-cat picked that moment to appear from nowhere, to rub silky fur against their legs.

Lucy smiled.

'I think the Tiger-cat is coming too!' But T-Tongue had the last word: 'WOOF!'